Clouds Tumbled into the Valley

I0629692

By Carl L. Engel

Philadelphia, Pennsylvania

First published by King Tide Press, 2025
King Tide Press is a registered trade name of
King Tide LLC, Philadelphia, Pennsylvania

www.kingtidepress.com

ISBN 979-8-9851497-5-3 ebook
ISBN 979-8-9851497-4-6 pbk.

Cover designed by Katarina of Serbia

Clouds Tumbled
into the Valley

PROLOGUE

The brakes of a school bus squealed as it rolled to a stop in the parking lot of the Pennsylvania Barbeque restaurant in Indiana, Pennsylvania. Its folding doors parted to release a class of sixth graders from Ben Franklin Elementary School who'd been invited by the Indiana County Historical Society to attend the dedication of a historical marker to an abolitionist who'd grown up nearby.

Under a clear and sunny sky, the children and their teachers stood huddled together against a cold wind in front of a tall, blue aluminum sign that had been provided by the Pennsylvania Historical and Museum Commission. Cars and trucks raced by, the sign having been erected several feet from the shoulder of Route 954. A podium had been set up beside it. After some welcoming remarks from a member of the Historical Society, the children sang "Lift Every Voice and Sing" by James Weldon Johnson.

Then came the event for which they all had gathered: The canvas was removed from the sign, unveiling its text. In bright yellow letters, it read:

1

ABSALOM (ALBERT) HAZLETT
(1837-1860)

— ♟ —

A staunch abolitionist, Hazlett became a
lieutenant in John Brown's provisional
army and participated in the raid on
Harper's Ferry Arsenal in 1859. He was
captured, tried, convicted, and hanged for
his involvement following the failed
Harper's Ferry attack. This incident,
intended to arm slaves to fight for their
own freedom, was a major catalyst for the
outbreak of the Civil War. Hazlett was
born and raised near here.

When the applause subsided, Dr. Catherine Catalfamo, a
professor of history at nearby St. Vincent College, wearing a
Civil War-era dress and bonnet, approached the podium.

ABSALOM (ALBERT) HAZLETT
(1837 - 1860)

A staunch abolitionist, Hazlett became a lieutenant in John Brown's provisional army and participated in the raid on Harper's Ferry Arsenal in 1859. He was captured, tried, convicted, and hanged for his involvement following the failed Harper's Ferry attack. This incident, intended to arm slaves to fight for their own freedom, was a major catalyst for the outbreak of the Civil War. Hazlett was born and raised near here.

I

The first leaves of the fall quivered in the wind and dropped, littering the towpath. Albert walked alongside two horses, guiding them with his riding crop. The taut rope that led to the canalboat behind them groaned as it tugged against the iron buckles of their harnesses. He felt a chill as they once again stepped out of the sunlight and into the shadow of another one of the Appalachians' steep forested valleys.

The melodious chirping of birds was interrupted by a shout from the boatman: "Hey, Al!"

Albert stopped and turned around. His colleague was leaning lazily against the rudder in his usual fashion. "You hungry!?" he asked.

Albert wasn't hungry, but a fire and a meal would interrupt his boredom from walking the same canal path that he'd been trodding for the past several years. The unseasonably cold day reminded him that winter would soon arrive, and with it bitter winds that would lash his face and strip the trees of their beauty. "Yeah!" he answered.

***

The flames of the campfire danced madly in the cold autumn breeze. The sun had already fallen behind the treetops, and its reflection gave the ripples on the narrow Conemaugh River a golden shimmer. In the near distance could be heard the roar of rushing water, as the lock through which they'd just passed emptied to accommodate another westward traveler.

Albert swirled the coffee in his mug. "How much is McGovern paying you for this trip?" he asked the boatman, before taking a sip.

"Why are you asking me that?"

"I've been working for the man for almost three years now, and I just want to know if he's treating me fairly. I deserve to know. There's no reason for you not to tell me."

"I assume it's the same amount as you, Al."

"And how much is that?"

The boatman thought for a moment. "Three dollars per day," he said.

"Three dollars!? So why am I only getting one-fifty for the same work?"

"He trusts me with the boat, Al. It's his asset."

"Trusts you my ass. You're just on the rudder because I'm the only one of the two of us who's any good with horses. Are you trying to tell me that the horses aren't assets, too?"

The boatman shrugged his shoulders as he gazed at the dancing flames.

***

Their stretch of the canal terminated at the Allegheny River where, at the Freeport wharf, the cargo would be transferred from canalboat to riverboat for the next leg to Pittsburgh. After they'd pulled the boat to the dock, Albert unhitched the horses and led them to a stable next to the tavern where he and the boatman, and seemingly every other canal worker at the junction, refreshed themselves at each turnaround. The boatman would meet him after the cargo had been unloaded and he'd collected the bills of lading from the riverboat captains and had supervised the loading of any cargo onto his and Albert's boat for the journey back to Johnstown. It usually took him half the day.

Albert didn't waste any time. He pulled an empty chair out from a table of cardplayers, stood on top of it, and declared to everyone present, "I have two horses and a canalboat for sale! If anyone's interested, I'll be sitting at the bar!"

His voice was barely louder than the din of drunken conversation and, aside from a few patrons who were staring at him blankly, he didn't seem to have generated any interest at all. Albert took a seat at the bar and ordered a beer, hoping at the very least that, if nobody was interested, none of them would tell the boatman about what he'd done.

But before he could start truly feeling sorry for himself, a man with long oily gray hair took a seat on the stool next to him. "How much do you want?" he asked.

"Seventy-five for the horses, and two hundred for the boat."

"I don't believe for a minute that you own those horses or that boat."

"I inherited them from my father."

"No, you didn't. Does your partner know that you're trying to sell the business?"

"He's not my partner. He works for me."

"Bullshit. But I'll tell you what: I'll give you twenty for the horses and fifty for the boat. I'm the one who's going to have to deal with your pissed-off friend, so I want a discount."

"He's not my friend, either."

"That I believe. What if he refuses to give me the boat?"

"I can give you the horses right away. What's he going to do with a canalboat and no horses to pull it?"

***

Albert's plan had been to grab a few items from the Hazlett farm in Indiana, whatever he could take that wouldn't be very much missed by his family, before fleeing Pennsylvania. But the sheriff, two mounted deputies, and John McGovern were already there, waiting with his father, Alexander, when he arrived, their eyes locking onto his as soon as he lifted his head to look up from the dusty road. His father had his arms folded across his chest and was wearing an expression that struck Albert as more accusatory than even that of the sheriff. The deputies sat alert on their horses, watching to see how Albert would react. He didn't try to run.

The sheriff and Alexander waited for him to draw close enough to hear them. Then, the sheriff spoke first. "Your coworker sent us a telegraph from Freeport before you even left town. I won't waste everyone's time by asking what you were thinking, because Mr. McGovern has been merciful enough to forbear from pursuing a criminal indictment if you apologize and return the money."

Alexander uncrossed his arms and pointed a finger at Albert's forehead. "I want you to know that I don't agree with John's approach, Absalom." He jabbed at the air with his finger as he spoke. "We didn't teach you to steal. We taught you that thieves and liars shall be cast into the lake of fire and brimstone, where the beast and false prophet are, to be tormented day and night for ever and ever. And so, too, should you be punished." He let his hand drop. "But John's a Catholic," he continued, his tone a trace softer, "and he sees things a little differently. As he's an old friend of mine, I'm not going to argue with him."

Albert turned to McGovern and apologized, then took the wad of bills from his pocket and handed it over.

"Seventy dollars!?" shouted McGovern with a smile as he counted the bills. "If I weren't so rich already, I'd be infuriated. But frankly I'm just amazed at what a terrible businessman you are."

"The prodigal son can always return, Absalom," said Alexander, "but he must first acknowledge his sins against God and family. I don't see anything like that from you. When I do, you can live here again."

"You're kicking me off the farm?"

"We've made it too easy for you, son. You need to learn to make your own way."

"The youths don't appreciate the value of a dollar," said McGovern, shaking his head and recounting the bills.

"But where am I supposed to go?" Albert pleaded, his plan to resettle elsewhere now having been frustrated by the sudden absence of money and provisions.

"The original prodigal son worked on a pig farm," answered his father. "That may be a good place to start."

II

The windows of the ironworks glowed fervently against the black shadow of the long mountain ridge that loomed behind it in the night. A fresh blanket of snow coated rooftops and the frozen river, and reflected the moonlight, casting the town in radiant silver. Smoke discharged from the stacks, blotting out stars and stinging Albert's hazel eyes. He'd never liked Johnstown, but there was work here.

As he did most evenings, he was eating dinner with his fellow millworkers, most of whom were Germans, in the town's beer hall. Stifled by the odor of sweat and alcohol, he'd come out to the balcony for a cigarette. Through the closed door behind him, he could still hear an accordion wheezing and a tuba honking in triple time, interrupted by fits of men's laughter and shouting.

"You look like you'd rather be anywhere but here."

Albert didn't recognize the voice, or the speaker's face when he turned to look at it. It was marked by deep wrinkles and bulbous papules that reminded Albert of a relief map of Pennsylvania he'd once seen as a boy. The old man's head was covered with a light gray stocking cap which matched the pallor of his skin and made his visage skeletal.

"Maybe so," Albert responded, "but I don't know how to

get anywhere different. I'm as broke as anyone else stuck working in this dump."

The old man nodded toward the door. "Those guys in there can't even speak English. They're stuck. You're not stuck. What'd you do before coming here?"

"Drove horses on the canal."

"That's good work. Why'd you stop?"

Albert sucked on his cigarette for a moment. "My employer went out of business," he said.

"If you're good with horses, I may have an opportunity for you." A faint smile flashed across the old man's lips. "You good with horses?"

"Yeah. I'm good with horses."

Albert flicked his cigarette butt into the muddy street, its spark extinguishing on contact, then followed the old man back inside.

***

"This fella tells me he's an equestrian," said the old man as he pulled an empty chair to a table where three others were seated, each one old enough to be Albert's father. He gestured with his palm for Albert to sit.

"You from around here?" asked a red-bearded man in a buckskin vest.

"Yessir. Indiana County."

"Then how come I've never seen you at the livestock auctions or horse shows?"

"I was driving a team on the canal. I didn't have time for auctions or shows."

The men at the table laughed, and Albert began to feel fear radiating from the old man's face. "Now Jim," said the old man to the one with the red beard, "remember that I warned you that the pickings here would be slim. Most of these guys don't even speak English."

Jim waved a hand gently to silence him. Albert's stomach turned as he tried to imagine why this trembling old codger

14

was so afraid of Jim, but he didn't see a reason to leave the table. He hated shoveling coal into a blast furnace, blisteringly hot and as blinding as the sun, while men shouted around him in languages he didn't understand.

"That's alright," said Jim. "He can learn on the job. That is, if he wants the job. Do you want to be a horse trader, son?"

"It's better than what I'm doing now," said Albert.

***

As they rode along the river in the predawn light, the only sound was the hooves of their horses against the frozen dirt road. Behind the wooded mountains ahead, a soft glow signaled the dawn. A frosty breeze nipped at Albert's face.

As the sun began to illuminate the mountaintops, they arrived at a farm with a small white house and a big red barn. The snow-covered fields were dotted with white lumps of buried hay bales.

"This is it, boys," said Jim.

The men dismounted. Two of them immediately began to remove rails on the wooden fence of the corral while Jim ran to the barn door with a hacksaw to saw off the padlock. Albert didn't dare ask where the farmer was, or why they needed to break into the stable.

He waited by the barn door with the others. The padlock dropped into the mud, and when the doors swung upon, the horses inside began to whinny and buck. The men scrambled to bridle all twelve of them, then tied them into four trains of three to be led to their destination. Before the sun had even cleared the eastern ridgeline, they were on the road north to New York.

***

The Chemung County Livestock Auction occupied a full block of stables and small corrals across the street from the railroad station in Elmira. Fumes from coal-fired engines

15

combined with the stink of manure to fill the air with a noxious, urban stench. Even though it was Albert's first time outside of his home state, forested Appalachian ridges hugged the town in a familiar way that allayed his feeling of estrangement.

The stockyard teemed with excitement. As an Irish string band fiddled and strummed over the thumping beats of an all-Black drum corps, the crowd, even those pushing each other for better views of the penned animals, seemed to rock and bounce to the rhythms rolling through them. Albert sipped on a mug of coffee and watched the concert while his two colleagues fielded questions from prospective bidders. Jim, meanwhile, was registering the horses at the auctioneer's office.

The guitar player was swaying his hips and singing a love ballad at a near wail. As Albert bobbed his head to the music, a heavy callused palm grabbed his shoulder and pulled him from his rapture.

It was one of his colleagues, who'd come to warn him that "the law is on the way over for a visit." He nodded at two young men with glinting seven-point stars on their chests, strolling along the stalls and inspecting the brand on each horse.

"I knew we should've rebranded them," said the other.

"It never looks good," said the first. "It always just looks like you're trying to cover up the old brand. It's better to just sell them before word gets out that they're missing." Then, after a pause, he said that he'd "better go tell Jim" and disappeared into the crowd.

Albert watched the sheriff's deputies work their way down the row. When they arrived at his stall, he noticed that his other colleague had slipped away, too, and he'd been left alone.

One of the deputies greeted him warmly. "Do you mind if we inspect the brands?" he asked. But the other had already started to do so, and before Albert could answer the question, both deputies were huddled next to a mare's buttock exchanging urgent whispers.

"Are these horses yours?" asked one of them.

"No," said Albert. "They're my boss's."

***

Sitting on the witness stand, Albert was reminded of the choirstall of the church where he'd sung as a boy. A congregation of spectators was crammed into pews in front of him, devouring his every word. He'd been testifying for several hours and felt a painful urge to use a latrine, but was much too afraid to say so. The judge loomed over his right shoulder, an expression of stern dispassion carved onto his stone face. Albert couldn't tell whether his eyes were open or closed.

"The prosecution told you that they'd set you free if you testified against my clients?" asked the attorney for the defendants. "Isn't that right?"

Albert looked at Jim and his two accomplices, all of them in new three-piece suits and wearing their hair slicked back like a coven of Pittsburgh bankers. The prosecutor's elbows were planted on the table as he pressed his hands together prayer-like, his lips firmly kissing the tips of his forefingers.

"No," Albert answered. "They told me that if I confessed, they would kick me out of New York instead of throwing me in jail. So, I confessed."

"They told you that you had to testify, too, didn't they?"

"Objection, Your Honor!" cried the prosecutor, rising to his feet. "The prosecution has compelled the witness to appear under our subpoena power to bring fact witnesses to testify at trial. There was no quid pro quo agreement as counsel suggests."

"The witness can answer for himself, counsellor," said the judge dryly. "Go ahead, Mr. Hazlett." The prosecutor sat back down and resumed his monastic pose.

"I was compelled by his subeaner power just like he said," Albert testified. He saw smiles creep across the faces of several in the gallery.

"And how much of the rest of your testimony was 'just like

17

he said?"" probed the defense attorney.

"Objection!" cried the prosecutor, again on his feet in an instant. "That's argumentative, Your Honor! The defense is suggesting that-"

The judge raised a hand to quiet the lawyer. "That's sustained," he said. Turning to the defense attorney, he continued, "You've made your point, counsellor. Is there anything else?"

There was not, and Albert was allowed to step down from the witness stand and to use a latrine. Once relieved, a sheriff's deputy led him to a jail cell to wait while the attorneys presented their closing arguments and the jury deliberated. He had to be held until the trial's close, the deputy explained, in case there was a mistrial and he had to testify again.

"I know that they told you to get the hell out of New York," said the deputy, "but you'd be smart to stay out of Pennsylvania, too. You saw the suits on those guys. Theirs isn't exactly a small operation. Understand?"

Albert nodded.

After several hours, they received word that the jury had found Jim and his accomplices guilty of attempting to sell stolen property, and that they would be extradited back to Pennsylvania to face trial for burglary and larceny.

The deputy escorted Albert to the train station and placed him on the next train to Johnstown. As the train departed, Albert smoked a cigarette on a gangway between two cars and watched the setting sun paint the sky red. Snowmelt trickled down the hillsides on either side of the track, and the branches of the trees were dotted with bright green buds. Spring had come while he'd been in jail.

III

"He's forgiven you, Absalom," said his mother, Sarah. "He wanted you to know that."

"I suppose I'll have to take your word on that."

Alexander, who was lying on the bed next to Sarah's rocking chair, coughed violently, his entire body contracting and kicking, flinging the blankets that had been covering him onto the floor. A doctor had told them that the cause was a build-up of dust from his work as a stone mason before he'd inherited their farm from his sister.

When the coughing fit subsided, Alexander began to groan.

"That means he wants water," said Sarah, showing no strain to get up from her seat. A cold rainstorm pattered against the window and rattled its panes behind her. The candle on the sill flickered in the draft.

Albert grabbed the tin mug on the bedside table and knelt by his father, using a spoon to drip water onto his tongue.

"He can't swallow," she said, "so don't give him too much."

Alexander began to cough again. Albert pulled the spoon away.

"What did I tell you?" she said.

After the fit had ended, Albert held another spoonful of water to his father's lips, but he just shook his head and closed his eyes.

"Shouldn't be long now," said Sarah.

***

Albert was hoping to eat his slice of funeral cake and drink his coffee in quiet when he stepped out to the porch, but his brother Jonas was already there, seated in one of the wicker armchairs and looking at him as though he'd been waiting for him to arrive.

"So, now what?" asked Jonas. "You getting out of here?" He grinned wryly. "Away from the great vengeance and furious rebukes of your horse-thieving gang?"

"That deputy was just trying to scare me."

"I'd sure be scared."

Albert shrugged. "Somebody has to stick around to help Mother with the picking," he said.

"Albert, just look at the field," said Jonas, gesturing at it with an open palm. "Hardly nothing got planted before Father got sick. Mother's going to have to hire you out to the neighbors just like you were last fall, and the fall before that, too."

"So, what's your big plan?"

"I've been rereading some of William's letters from Kansas," he began, referring to their eldest brother, who'd moved with his wife several years earlier to Bourbon County, at the border with Missouri, and had kept in regular correspondence with the family ever since. "And the way he describes it, with every tree that is pleasant to the sight and good for food, every beast of the field, and every fowl of the air... I can't stand the feeling of being stuck here imagining it when I know it to be real. I think that you should come with me, Al. What do you say?"

The front door whipped open and out stuck their mother's head. "Albert, Jonas, get back in the house. We have guests. You're embarrassing me."

Albert sighed heavily. "Okay, I'll go," he said, looking at

Jonas.

"You mean you'll 'come,'" said Sarah.

"Sure, that too."

Sarah squinted at Albert quizzically for a moment, then shook her head. "Don't dawdle," she said, turning back inside.

"Believe me, I won't," he said as she closed the door behind her, ignoring his response. Jonas's grin was so wide that Albert feared his cheeks might burst.

IV

Leafy branches and tall, yellow grass waved in the breeze on either side of the border all the same. Though unseen, a product of politician's imaginations and surveyor's instruments, its presence was as real as a witch's curse, disturbing the atmosphere and conjuring chaos out of tranquility. Albert had sensed the transition in the gazes of the men whom they'd passed along the road. Though their eyes had long reflected ever more aversion and suspicion the further west they'd travelled, the sight of a stranger now sparked flashes of hostility and distrust. By the time he'd seen the first sign confirming their arrival in Kansas Territory, painted on the side of a stagecoach station near Fort Scott, he'd felt lightning in his spine and thunder in his belly, as though being there were an adventure in itself.

William's farm was near Coal Centre, a ramshackle hamlet of simple wooden structures and muddy lanes that could've been mistaken for a single farmstead, if not for the towering iron derricks that marked the mineshafts on its outskirts. In one of the buildings was a general store where a few tables had been arranged in the back for men to drink their purchases on the premises, and it was here, several months after his arrival and after an autumn spent harvesting corn for his brother, that

Albert first met James Montgomery.

He approached as Albert was sitting alone and staring blankly at the pint of beer set before him. "What you're looking for isn't in that glass," he said. His tall, slender figure cast a narrow shadow across the center of the table. On account of the flecks of gray in his hair and the wrinkles under his eyes, Albert surmised that he was well into his forties.

"I'm not looking for anything," Albert replied. "This glass of beer just happens to be the prettiest thing here."

"Do you like working your brother's land?"

"How do you know who I am?"

"This isn't a big place, Albert." He pulled out a chair and seated himself, then signaled the shopkeeper for a drink.

"I don't like picking or plowing any more than anyone else," Albert answered.

The shopkeeper set a glass of beer in front of Montgomery, who immediately drank half of it in one long swig. So much foam coated his bushy moustache, and so many droplets dribbled down his long beard, that Albert wondered how much of it actually had made it down the man's throat.

"You know anything about horses?" Montgomery asked as he set his glass back down on the table.

Albert paused for a moment before answering. Studying the man's eyes, he saw creases in the corner which hinted at a smile under all of those whiskers. "Something tells me that you already know the answer to that," he said.

"You're famous in New York," said Montgomery with a laugh. "Infamous, I guess it would be," correcting himself. "Quite a few people who've come here from there know who you are."

Albert felt his face melt into a frown.

"You can't run away from your problems, son," continued Montgomery, his voice now syrupy with paternalism, "because you can't run away from who you are. But if you are who they say you are, then I've got an opportunity for you. Are you who they say you are?"

Albert pondered the question for a moment, then finished

his beer in a single gulp and set his glass back on the table with a knock. "I guess you'll have to find out," he said.

***

Fort Scott had no walls, batteries, or other defenses to protect it. Formerly an outpost used by the military to police local Indians, it consisted of a dozen large, two-story buildings arranged around a central courtyard; two cylindrical brick buildings at its center, one of which had been a magazine and the other still housing a well; and a long stable which marked its northwest boundary. Scattered around the complex were the shops and houses of pro-slavery settlers who'd moved there after the fort had been decommissioned several years earlier. In the twilight of early morning, these structures, monochrome gray against a field of fresh white snow, looked to Albert from a distance like tombstones.

With Montgomery at the lead, the seventy riders proceeded at a trot, careful not to awaken the inhabitants. As he'd done before every one of their raids, Montgomery had briefed his troops on the task at hand: Benjamin Rice, who'd been convicted of stealing horses and killing a pro-slavery supporter the previous winter, was being held in a cell on the third floor of the old fort building that had been turned into the Fort Scott Hotel, and they were going to break him out.

Once they'd arrived within a hundred yards of it, they dismounted. Ten of them, including a talkative young man named John Cook, were selected to guard the horses and the twelve-pound howitzer that they'd brought with them, which had been seized in an earlier raid.

Everyone else, including Albert, crept across the field to the hotel's veranda, snow creaking under their boots as they walked. When they reached the front door, they gathered in a semicircle around Montgomery, who kicked it in without hesitation. Almost immediately, lamps began to illuminate windows in nearly every building of the settlement, and the panicked barking of men erupted from inside the hotel. Albert and a few others were ordered to wait outside and guard the door.

"We need an axe!" shouted John Kagi, a young lawyer from Ohio who'd been active with Montgomery's militia for several years. He was promptly provided with one by a boy named William Leeman, the youngest member of their group. Minutes later, Rice, still shackled to a broken chain, emerged to cheers.

As the freed prisoner was making his way through the crowd, thanking his rescuers and shaking their hands, two gunshots rang out from a hardware store across the square. Albert's arm burned, as though he'd been branded with an iron. When he looked at it, he saw a crimson splotch spreading over his sleeve. Blood dripped onto the snow.

"I'm hit!" he cried.

One of the others, a portly old man, rushed over and quickly cut open Albert's shirt to examine the injury. "It only grazed you," he said, not without concern. He called for some whiskey and a bandage.

Albert winced against the sting of the alcohol and turned away from the dressing of his wound. Lying in the snow a few yards away, surrounded by several others crouching and kneeling, someone appeared to have been gravely injured. Albert heard Montgomery and his lieutenants shout orders, then watched the militiamen hurry to surround the store. After a few exchanges of gunfire, a white flag was hung from a window and the surrender of the occupants was accepted. The shopkeeper shouted that his son had just been killed in the shootout, and he'd lost the will to continue fighting. Though his life was spared, his property was not, and his store was promptly swarmed by the raiders.

Dawn broke and the snowy plain began to shine, reflecting the brilliant sun. As Albert watched the looting, he rested his bandaged arm on top of his head, as the portly man had advised, and fought off sleep and prayed not to die. He sat like that, leaned back against the wheel of the howitzer, for several hours while Montgomery's men packed everything up and prepared to leave.

V

Montgomery led Albert and the few dozen other militiamen who hadn't returned to their homes after leaving Fort Scott thirty miles north to "Fort Snyder." No more than a few hundred yards from the border, its elevation and natural earthen ramparts made the location well suited for staging raids into Missouri and repelling incursions into Kansas Territory. These benefits, however, were ancillary to its purpose: The "fort," a single stone house, had been erected as a memorial. In a dale cut into the middle of the hills there, five free-state settlers had been executed by a gang of pro-slavery raiders the spring before, in what journalists had called "the Marais de Cygnes Massacre," taking the name from a nearby river. John Brown and his militia soon thereafter built the house there and named it after Charles Snyder, who'd survived being shot in his leg and back during the attack.

They'd sat Albert by the kitchen fireplace to keep him warm while they dressed his wound properly. Heavy with whiskey, the warmth of the hearth, and the discharge of adrenaline, he drifted in and out of sleep. Hazy figures flitted in the blur beneath his drooping eyelids, unrecognizable save for their host. Gray-haired and pale-eyed, raw-boned and gaunt-cheeked, and stooping slightly, his nearly six-foot frame seemed to angle over the others. His clothes were stiff and poorly tailored and hung from his body no differently than they'd hung from the racks at the haberdashery. If Albert had been more delirious, he might've thought that he was looking at a scarecrow that had come to life. But the man's fluffy white beard is what gave him away; that's how Albert knew that he was looking at John Brown.

"For, lo, the wicked bend their bow," he said as he handed Albert a mug of coffee. "They make ready their arrow upon the string, that they may privily shoot at the upright in heart." A smile curled across his lips as he continued, "Or in the arm, as it were." Then, looking into Albert's eyes, he asked, "If the foundations be destroyed, what can the righteous do?"

He knew that Brown was quoting scripture from having grown up with Alexander for a father, but he had no recollection of the answer to this question. "Pray to God, sir?" he ventured safely.

"You're wise beyond your years, son," said Brown with a wink. "For the righteous Lord loveth righteousness, and his countenance doth behold the upright."

Albert could scarcely imagine that this warm giver of hot drink on a cold night was the man rumored to have led his sons to slaughter five pro-slavery settlers at Pottawatomie Creek two years earlier. As he searched for something to say, Brown gave him a gentle pat on the knee, then went to continue assisting the others with preparations for their next raid.

***

The militia would be returning south, halfway back to Fort Scott, to the Little Osage River, Montgomery briefed the men as they were eating dinner several nights later. The river ran west to east across the border until, thirty miles inside Missouri, it converged with the Marais de Cygnes to form the Osage River. That thirty-mile stretch of the Little Osage between the border of Kansas Territory and the source of the Osage was dotted with slave-holding settlements, and it was their mission

28

to liberate these slaves and deliver them to Canada.

It was announced that the group would split at the raid's conclusion, with Brown leading the freed slaves to Canada and Montgomery returning to Kansas Territory. When Brown asked for volunteers for his expedition, Albert, his fork in his good hand, raised his wounded arm as high as he could, wincing in pain. Brown's confidence and piety had kindled a passion in Albert, who now found himself wanting to do more than steal horses for Montgomery's militia.

***

As Albert and the other riders set out for the Little Osage, the sun was setting behind them, gilding the treetops and tinting the clouds pink and orange. By the time they'd crossed the border, the sky was illuminated only by the faint silver glow of a crescent moon. They travelled southeast along the Marais de Cygnes, concealed in the shadows of the skeletal silhouettes of the leafless trees that lined the riverbanks for hundreds of feet on either side, their branches clawing at Albert's jacket and scratching at his face. At the Miami Creek tributary, the men turned south, then rode for another half hour at a canter until they reached the banks of the Little Osage.

As they approached the first plantation at a gallop, Albert saw a lantern light up in one of the farmhouse windows. When they reached the gate of the picket fence that surrounded it, one of Brown's lieutenants, a sleepy-eyed army deserter named Aaron Stevens, dismounted and asked for someone to accompany him. Aaron had served as a cavalryman in the U.S. Dragoons, policing Indian territories along the Rocky Mountains until he'd bludgeoned a superior officer with a bugle in Taos and had been sent to Fort Leavenworth in Kansas Territory for a court martial. Certain that he'd be executed otherwise, he'd escaped to Topeka, where he'd been recruited into Brown's militia on account of his military experience.

Albert had seen that his tranquil visage concealed a

29

simmering intensity that boiled to the surface in unpredictable bursts. To be in his presence gave Albert the same thrill as a boat ride down the Allegheny River, its long winding current interrupted by rapids that seemed always to appear in the blind curves, hidden behind the tree-lined slopes of its serpentine ravines. His pull on Albert had been magnetic ever since they'd met at Fort Snyder, and Albert was quick to join him on this errand.

Aaron knocked on the front door and announced that they were there to free the young woman who was being kept there as a slave. To Albert's surprise, the proprietor opened the door and let them in. Brown and the others remained on their horses outside.

"Sie ist hinten," said the proprietor to Aaron. "Kommen Sie, bitte."

As Aaron followed him into a back room, his wife shouted at them, "Nein! Nein! Nein! Raus! Raus hier!"

Albert stepped behind her, wrapped an arm around her chest, and held his revolver against her temple. With him and Aaron both occupied, the homeowners' young son unlatched the back door and sprinted across the short yard and into the thick woods behind the house. Then, a gunshot.

"Aaron!?" shouted Albert. The woman in his arms went stiff with fear.

"I'm alright," he answered. "The old German I'm not so sure about."

The woman began to wail, and Albert let her drop to the floor. He would read several months later in a newspaper that the dead man's name had been David Crews.

A young Black woman stood in the front doorway, gazing wide-eyed at Brown and the other mounted liberators.

"Stand fast therefore in the liberty wherewith Christ hath made us free, and be not entangled again with the yoke of bondage!" Brown declared to her. "Come along!"

Without speaking a word, she turned back into the house to gather her possessions.

Albert, meanwhile, went to the stables as he always did, this time with a gangly young man named Charles Tidd, who had blond hair that covered his ears. There were only six horses, making their work quick and simple. Albert and Charles each led three on a line behind them as they rode at the back of the group. The raid would continue to another three homesteads, freeing ten more slaves and yielding another eight horses, a mule, and three wagons. But Albert's work was already done; his hands were full.

The militia crossed back into Kansas Territory just ten miles north of Fort Scott. They'd made a complete loop since the raid there a week before, and Albert was beginning to feel as though his purpose was becoming as circuitous as his forays into Missouri. He imagined that the journey to Canada would provide a new opportunity at adventure.

He guided the horses to where Montgomery was sipping on a steaming mug of coffee as he stared down at a pale young man with dark hair named Jeremiah Anderson, who was cooking bacon and eggs over a fire.

"I wanted to hand over the spoils to you personally," said Albert, offering the reins to Montgomery, "as a token of my appreciation."

"I don't think his ambitions end in Canada," said Montgomery. Albert was surprised by the absence of a smile or any other hint of gratitude for his gesture. Montgomery's eyes narrowed, "That's a warning, son."

"Where do you think he's going after Canada?" asked Albert.

"I suspect that he thinks he's going to Calvary, but I can't claim to know where he'll actually end up." He took another sip from his mug, then added, "Christ dies in the end, son. Don't you forget it."

"But he came back. He resurrected."

"He might've. But will you?"

VI

While several from Brown's militia ventured south to Topeka to resupply, Albert and Aaron rode north to scout a passage into Nebraska Territory. Several days of warm temperatures had melted the snow and turned the muddy creeks that web across the plains of northern Kansas into brown torrents. The two riders were following Straight Creek's meandering course through the high, rolling hills in search of a place where they could ford the wagons, when, upon rounding yet another bend, they spotted eight U.S. marshals watering their horses. The bare winter foliage offered them nowhere to hide.

"We'd better keep it moving," said Albert. "If we turn around now, they'll think we're running from something."

Aaron didn't respond, but just continued at a trot as though he'd already made the same decision. When they were within earshot, he waved at the soldiers. A few of them waved back. The lead marshal, or so it seemed by the way he outdressed the others, stepped out to greet them.

"You fellas seen any Negroes around here?" he asked.

"No," thought Albert. They would easily be on their way.

"Yes," said Aaron.

Albert looked at him blankly, struggling to figure out what

he was thinking. After a moment, he just turned slowly back to the officer and nodded his head.

"Where'd you see them Negroes?" asked the marshal.

"I don't know the name of the place, sir," said Aaron. "But I can show it to you."

Albert closed his eyes, hoping that his ancestors, Jesus, or anyone else might tell him just what the hell was going on. When he opened them, the others were mounting their horses for the ride back to the little cabin in Holton where the fugitives were waiting with Brown and the rest of their escort for the Topeka detachment to return with the provisions needed for the next leg of their journey.

When the cabin was in view, Aaron said, "They're in there. Just a couple of 'em. Some women."

When they were about fifty feet from the front porch, he was the first to dismount. Then, he drew his revolver. "Come on," he said. "I'll show you." He looked at Albert. "I'll need you to come along, too. There's only two of 'em, but you never know."

The lead marshal watched Aaron with squinted eyes, as though he were trying to decipher his ruse. So was Albert. But in the presence of the marshals, he was afraid to argue or to ask questions. He dismounted and drew his revolver, just like Aaron had done.

"Why don't you bring them out to us?" suggested the lead marshal.

"Alright," said Aaron. "But can you give us an armed guard? That way we'd have 'em outnumbered." Albert noticed that he was now speaking more loudly, almost shouting.

The lead marshal hesitated a moment, but then nodded his head gently and ordered one of his deputies to accompany them. As they approached the door, the deputy walked behind them. Albert felt his gaze burning into his neck.

They stepped onto the porch and Aaron said, "I've never cleared a room before, sir. Do I just, like, kick in the door?"

"I'll do it," said the deputy. He pounded his fist against the front door. "U.S. marshals!" he shouted. Albert heard a quiver

34

in his voice.

One of the young women they'd freed shouted from inside, "It's unlocked!"

The deputy pursed his lips and appeared to think for a moment. He looked behind him at the other seven marshals, exhaled sharply, then turned the doorknob to enter.

When the door swung open, Brown's militiamen had ten guns trained on him. He simply froze, speechless. Aaron took the deputy's pistol and went back out to the porch.

"We've got your boy!" he shouted at the marshals. Then, turning around, he said, "Show 'em our prize, Al!"

Albert held his revolver to the deputy's head as one of Brown's sons, Owen, held his hands behind his back and pushed him onto the threshold for his colleagues to see. Several militiamen opened the cabin windows and aimed their rifles at the marshals.

The lead marshal appeared to shout an order to the others, too far away for Albert to hear, and the seven of them turned their horses around and tore off at a gallop in the direction of Fort Leavenworth.

"Are you going to kill me?" the deputy asked him.

***

That evening, the men who'd gone to Topeka returned with supplies, more horses, and about twenty new volunteers. Brown ordered that they depart at sunrise, before the marshals could return with reinforcements.

The wagons crawled through the slushy mud, pushed by the men as much as pulled by the horses. Owen Brown dutifully attended to his father, ensuring that his wagon maintained the lead. Albert wondered whether they would've been better off facing the marshals from behind the walls of the cabin.

When they reached Straight Creek, Albert noticed that it was flowing higher and more rapidly than the day before, and even then, he and Aaron hadn't been able to find a safe place to cross it.

"Oh, God," said John Brown, loud enough for all to hear, "In the multitude of thy mercy hear me, in the truth of thy salvation. Deliver me out of the mire and let me not sink. Let me be delivered from them that hate me, and out of the deep waters." He then ordered the men to prepare to ford the creek where they were.

As the men were picking and shoveling the streambank to make a ramp for the wagons, their prisoner began to wave his arms and rave like a lunatic. "Hey boys! I'm over here!" he shouted. "I'm over here! Hey boys!"

Albert looked to where the prisoner was facing and saw a stream of marshals on horseback winding through the brush along the banks on the opposite side. There must've been about seventy or eighty of them, by his estimate. He recognized the lead marshal from the day before, though he was no longer riding at the fore of the group.

"By the authority of the President of the United States of America," shouted one of them, "I order you to surrender yourselves to face charges of murder, larceny, and violations of the Fugitive Slave Law!"

"The thief cometh not, but for to steal, and to kill, and to destroy!" Brown shouted back at the marshal. "I am come that they might have life, and that they might have it more abundantly!"

He turned his horse around and spoke to the fugitives and his men. "Come on, let us deal wisely with them," he said, "lest they multiply, and it come to pass, that, when there falleth out any war, they join also unto our enemies, and fight against us." He paused for a moment, looked across the stream, and finished in a thundering voice, "And so get them up out of the land!" Then, he drew his sword from his scabbard, pointed it northward across the stream, and shouted, "Charge!"

Albert began to whoop and holler, riding alongside Aaron as they drove their horses together through the waist-deep water and up the opposite bank. When Albert reached the other side, he felt nearly certain that, with them being outnumbered four to one, he would emerge from the

36

streambed to find himself staring down the barrel of a marshal's rifle. But instead, when his horse climbed the opposite bank, he saw the rearends of the enemy as they raced back east, with several of those who'd lost their horses running after their colleagues, shouting for them to wait.

"We've got 'em on the run, boys!" shouted Aaron. He took off at a gallop to rout the marshals, and Albert, not willing to be left behind from an adventure, rode after him along with several of their confederates. Before they returned to the wagon train, they seized five horses and captured four more prisoners.

"I was hoping you'd rescue me," said the original captive upon meeting the new arrivals, "not keep me company."

They looked too exhausted and forlorn to retort, but they certainly weren't laughing. Restrained with their own wrist shackles, the marshals were lined at the center of the procession of wagons, people, and horses for the long march into Nebraska Territory. But when they reached the village of Sabetha, just a few miles south of the border, Brown set the captives free.

"Stand ye in the ways," he said, "and see, and ask for the old paths, where is the good way."

The marshals looked at him with no more expression than a blink. But Brown was incensed, blue flames dancing in his gaze. He raised his voice to a boom: "And walk therein, and ye shall find rest for your souls!"

The marshals stood there for a few moments, until Albert shouted at them, "You heard the man! He said 'walk!' So, get walking!"

They did so, and when they were out of view, Brown led his procession out of Kansas Territory.

***

Fog crept from the river and enveloped the Old Capitol Building, slowly pushing up the muddy avenue to where Albert stood on the porch outside a theater. The streetlamps glowed like stars, their posts having been obscured in the mist. He scanned between the nebulous orbs of light for whatever else was hidden there. The other men guarding the door with him fidgeted and paced, grumbling about marshals and spies. A cheer erupted from inside as Brown harangued another audience on his impromptu speaking tour across Iowa.

This was their fourth night in Iowa City, and word must've spread that Brown was in town giving lectures, because a small protest had gathered at the bottom of the front stairs. A couple of the protesters held banners made of bed sheets with slogans painted on them. "Thou Shalt Not Steal!" read one. "Missouri Murderers!" read another. The raid along the Little Osage had become national news. Albert clutched his rifle across his chest and watched the creeping fog wrap the protesters in ghostly haze.

Another cheer erupted from inside the theater, this time long and rollicking, signaling the end of the performance. The front doors burst open, and the audience spilled across the porch and onto the muddy street, most of them turning toward the river and disappearing into the fog. Soon Brown emerged with Aaron and the others in their group who'd been assigned to serve as bodyguards inside, including two brothers who'd just been recruited the day before named Edwin and Barclay Coppoc. From among the protesters, a short and stocky man of about thirty climbed onto a barrel and shouted at the crowd.

"The man from the prophesies, ladies and gentlemen! The demon that the prophet John revealed to us!" Turning to Brown, he said, "I know scripture, too, old timer!"

Brown stopped on the steps of the porch to watch the speaker, expressing no emotion.

"For such are false apostles, deceitful workers, transforming themselves into the apostles of Christ!" the man shouted at Brown. "And no marvel, for Satan himself is transformed into an angel of light! Therefore, it is no great thing if his ministers also be transformed as the ministers of righteousness, whose end shall be according to their works!"

He turned back down to the audience that had gathered

38

around his barrel. "This man is a thief and a murderer, who kills in the dark of night and has never known a fair fight. The thief cometh not, but for to steal, and to kill, and to destroy. So, I beseech you, brethren, mark them which cause divisions and offences contrary to the doctrine which ye have learned, and avoid them. For they that are such serve not our Lord Jesus Christ, but their own belly, and by good words and fair speeches deceive the hearts of the simple. And while your obedience is known by all, and I am glad therefore on your behalf, I still want you to be wise as to that which is good, and simple concerning evil. And the God of peace shall bruise Satan under your feet shortly." Looking again at Brown, he said, "The grace of our Lord Jesus Christ be with you. Amen."

Everyone watched Brown in silence, bracing for the storm of words that was certain to erupt. Albert felt his heart begin to race and the hairs on his arm standing on end. He knew of nobody with a keener knowledge of scripture than John Brown, and was certain that his response would eviscerate the speaker and expose his deceit.

Brown slowly descended the porch stairs and walked toward his antagonist, who'd climbed down from his barrel. Then, he drew two revolvers from the holsters on his hip to gasps from the crowd. Albert's jaw fell open as he watched the scene unfold, unsure of whether to intervene. But before any violence erupted, Brown handed the guns to the speaker and said, "You talk quite bravely, my friend. You will never have a better chance to shoot Old Brown as you do right now. So, do as you may."

The speaker squinted his eyes in confusion, looking back at Brown. "I'm not going to shoot you, old timer," he said. "I'm not the murderer here." Then, he handed back the guns and disappeared into the crowd.

The fog grew thick, and Albert watched it envelop those who remained. Unable to see more than two feet in front of him, he followed the laughter and voices of Brown, Aaron, and the others into the murk beyond the glow of the streetlamps and back to their camp.

The black silhouette of a tall wooden grain elevator against the starlit sky marked the group's destination: the railroad depot in Muscatine County, Iowa. There was no town there, just the towering elevator, a train station, a warehouse, and a few sheds. A chain of railcars stretched along a track, detached from a locomotive and waiting to be filled with goods brought down from Minneapolis to be transported across the Mississippi River and onward to Chicago. The dark shadows of the gaps between the cars reminded Albert of the rings on a milk snake, laying still and outstretched, digesting its belly full of field mice. A sympathetic railroad worker had arranged passage in one of the boxcars for Brown and the fugitives.

"I'm going to need you in Pennsylvania," Brown told Albert, as they stood gathered in front of its open door. "I'll know where to find you. I'll send you word when it's time for our foray into Harpers Ferry."

All that Albert had heard was that he was being sent back to the farm.

"I can't go back there," he said. He felt his heart drop into his stomach as he thought about what his mother would say when she opened the door to find him on her front porch. He couldn't tell her the truth about his participation in the raid at the Little Osage and his flight from Kansas Territory, and she would sense that he was lying and would assume that it was to conceal failure.

"Please don't make me go," he pleaded, hating the way his voice sounded.

"Don't worry, son. I come quickly. Hold that fast which thou hast, that no man take thy crown."

"I can go back to Kansas and meet you there," Albert offered.

"I'm not going back to Kansas. I'm going to the Northeast, to fundraise. And I can't have an entourage when I require inconspicuity."

Albert nodded softly.

Brown smiled. "The time is at hand," he said. "I come quickly. And my reward is with me, to give every man according as his work shall be."

Just as the rising sun lit the top of the grain elevator, Albert spotted a railyard worker walking along the row of cars toward the group. Brown greeted the man with a wave, and Albert watched as he and the fugitive slaves were ushered into the open boxcar and the door was rolled closed behind them, slamming shut with a metallic clank.

With nowhere else to go, Albert walked to the end of the railyard where he hid in some brush next to the tracks and waited for a locomotive to attach to the train. By the time it did, the sun was high overhead and the gaps between the cars no longer looked to Albert like the rings on a milk snake. He was able to see them clearly, and climbed into one at a run as the train rolled past. At the railyard in Chicago, he didn't look for Brown. He just found another eastbound train and made his way back to Pennsylvania.

VII

"I knew this day would come," said Sarah, as she stood in the doorway of their farmhouse. "Don't say I didn't warn you, Absalom. 'You'll never make it on your own,' I said. You're just not that kind of man."

She stepped to the side to allow him to cross the threshold, then followed behind as he walked to the bedroom that he used to share with his brothers.

"I'll clean out a drawer for you," she said as he stood dumbstruck by the door. In the year since he and Jonas had left, she'd already removed the bunkbeds and one of the two dressers, and had replaced them with a sewing table and a bed for guests – like him.

"I don't intend to stay very long," he said without turning around to face her.

"You didn't intend to be here in the first place."

Albert set his small bundle of possessions on the floor, leaned his rifle against a wall, and sat on the bed.

"I'll remind you that this isn't a charity house," said his mother. "You'll have to work to earn your keep."

"I didn't expect to find charity here."

After he'd settled in, Albert went out to the porch and looked at the dry, brown field sprinkled with light-gray rocks,

43

like salt on a pretzel. It was impossible for him to imagine growing even hay in that dirt, let alone corn, but at least the plowing and planting would keep him in room and board, and outside of the house, through the spring.

***

By mid-May, the field was littered with leafy little tufts that would grow over the summer into tall stalks of corn. It was more than Albert had expected, but meager in comparison to the neighbors' fields covered in bright green plants.

He was sitting on the porch with his feet on the rail, drinking his morning coffee and watching a doe and her fawn nibbling on leaves at the field's far end. On his lap was one of the old newspapers he'd borrowed from the reading room at his church. Brown had reached Canada with all eleven of the rescued slaves, plus a baby born along the way, Albert read, crossing the Detroit River into Windsor, Ontario, by ferry. The baby had been given the name "John Brown."

The front door creaked and Sarah stomped out, floorboards squealing beneath her.

"If you read the Bible as much as those damned newspapers," she said, "you might have some direction in your life, instead of just wandering around in circles until you've run out of money and have to come home to your mother. I can't baby you forever, Absalom. I'm an old woman."

"I have a plan, Mom. I'll be out of here before you know it."

"You've been saying that for months, Absalom, yet here you remain. So, you might as well keep yourself useful. The chicken coop needs mending. There's wire in the shed."

"Alright," he agreed.

The door slammed as she went back inside. The deer popped up their heads at the sound, then darted into the trees behind them.

That evening, after dinner, Albert sat at the writing desk next to the fireplace and wrote a message to Brown: "I wish it would come off soon, for I am tired of doing nothing."

The next morning, he sealed it in an envelope addressed to Brown's farm in North Elba, New York, then rode his horse to a post office in the next county just to make the errand take longer.

**

By the end of July, some of the neighbors had early corn to harvest. Albert wasn't bothered to be picking their fields instead of his own, where his mother was the overseer. But as he snapped ears from their stalks that day in the same neighbor's field that he'd worked ever since he was a boy, he felt a cold, hard core of fear and dread growing in his chest and mashing his heart and lungs into his ribcage. His mind raced with horrifying memories of the blast furnace at Johnstown, the pair of old mules pulling a half-empty boat down the canal, and Sarah looking at him with gleeful contempt, having been right about her son all along.

A flock of songbirds scattered from the trees at the edge of the field, and Albert walked through the corn, trying to see what had scared them away. He'd expected to find deer, but it was a young man with a leather satchel slung across his shoulder, beating against his hip in rhythm with his brisk steps.

"Your mother said that I could find you here," he said by way of greeting. "She didn't want to pay the two cents for delivery."

Albert didn't have any money on him, so they walked to his neighbor's farmhouse where he asked for an advance on his paycheck, which was granted. Then, he took the envelope from the courier and tore it open. It was from Brown. He was finally being summoned.

"Hey!" he shouted after the courier, who was already walking toward the road. "Where's Chambersburg!?"

"Franklin County! Down by Maryland!"

Two days on horseback from Harpers Ferry, Albert realized. He regretted having asked.

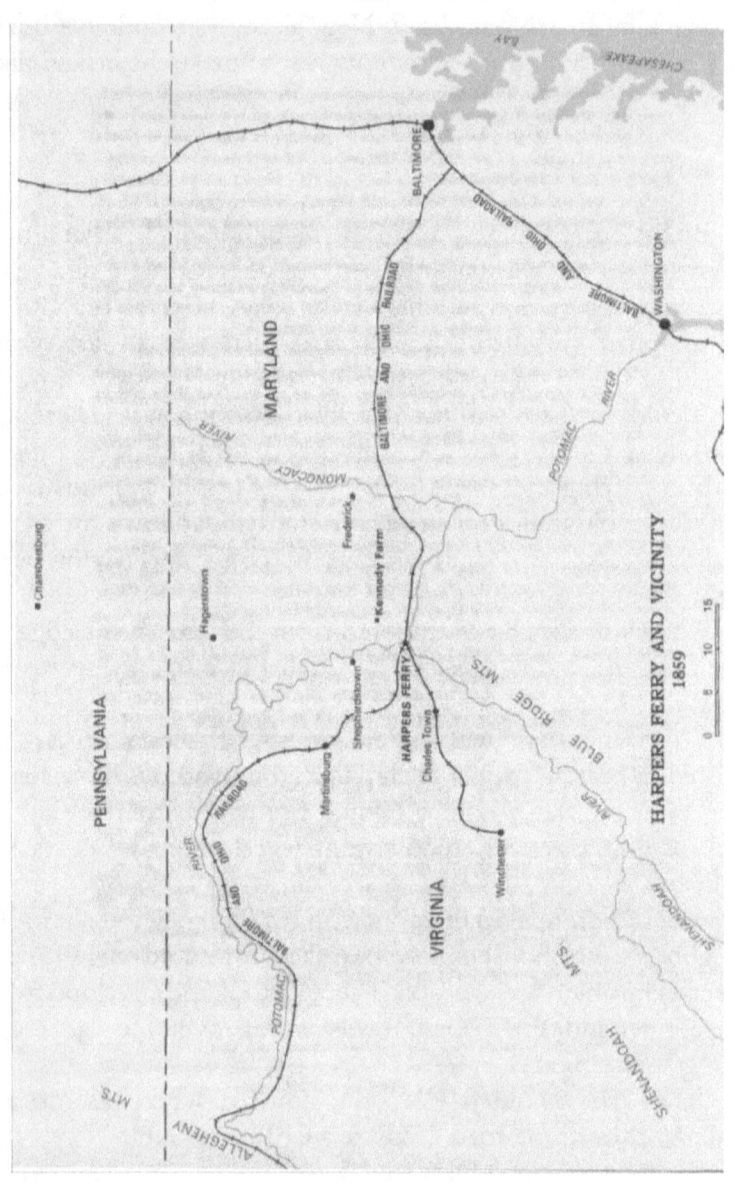

HARPERS FERRY AND VICINITY
1859

0   5   10   15

CHESAPEAKE BAY

BALTIMORE

WASHINGTON

BALTIMORE AND OHIO RAILROAD

BALTIMORE AND OHIO RAILROAD

MARYLAND

POTOMAC RIVER

MONOCACY RIVER

Frederick

Kennedy Farm

Hagerstown

Chambersburg

PENNSYLVANIA

Shepherdstown

HARPERS FERRY

Martinsburg

Charles Town

Winchester

VIRGINIA

BLUE RIDGE MTS

SHENANDOAH RIVER

SHENANDOAH MTS

BALTIMORE AND OHIO RAILROAD

POTOMAC RIVER

ALLEGHENY MTS

VIII

Sweat had soaked through Albert's shirt, and the strap of his heavy canvas duffel bag pulled on his neck, forcing his head down. The hot summer sun had baked the grass along the sidewalk into a light brown. Behind him, the clangs and squeals of iron on iron reverberated from the railyard from which he'd come, having hopped a train in Johnstown to Harrisburg, then another down the Cumberland Valley to Chambersburg.

At the massive two-story, red-brick prison on the corner of King Street, inmates were pressing their faces against the bars, yearning for the relief of a glancing breeze. There, he turned the corner and saw right away what Brown had described in his letter: a white clapboard house with three windows across the second story, and two to the left of a front door on the first. When he approached to knock, he saw a little sign on the wall that read "Ritner Boarding House."

The door was opened by the host, Mary Ritner, who looked a few years younger than his mother. She greeted him with warm eyes, as though she pitied what she saw.

"My name's Albert Hazlett, ma'am," he said. The way she was looking at him made him feel embarrassed.

"I know it is, baby," she said slowly, like she was soothing a skittish horse. "We've been expecting you."

She led him to the parlor, where a young man not much older than him was leaning over a map and sipping pensively on a pipe. Hearing them enter, he abandoned his thoughts to look at Albert, then, breaking into a wide grin, opened his arms to embrace him. It was John Kagi, his old friend from Montgomery's militia in Kansas Territory.

Kagi nodded toward the map. "You should look at this," he said. "It's where you're going tomorrow." He pointed at a red dot in Maryland, just south of where Antietam Creek flowed into the Potomac River, which marked what he called the "Kennedy Farm," named after the woman from whom Brown had rented it. "That's where he is right now," said Kagi, "making preparations." Seven miles down the road from there, and across a covered railroad bridge, was the United States Armory and Arsenal at Harpers Ferry.

"What happens after we take the armory?" asked Albert.

Kagi stared at the map for a moment, sipping on his pipe. "It's a revolution, Al," he said finally, smoke pouring from his mouth and nose as he spoke. "The armory will serve as our base of operations. First, we'll liberate slaves in the Cumberland Valley and bring them into our army, then the Shenandoah Valley, and then we'll push east across Virginia to the Chesapeake."

The plan sounded alright to Albert. After all, Kagi was a lawyer, and he and Brown had been planning the operation ever since their adventures in Kansas Territory.

"Follow me," said Kagi, as he pushed past Albert and started up the stairs. At one of the thresholds in the second-floor hallway, he stopped and said, "This is your bed for the night."

On the floor of the bedroom were several long crates with the word "furniture" painted on top of each one. Albert, struggling to imagine a piece of furniture that could fit inside, watched as Kagi pried one of them open with the back of a hammer to reveal brand new long-bore breech-loading rifles from the Sharps Company. Kagi also opened a box labelled "preserves" that contained ammunition, and another box

48

labelled "preserves" that actually contained jarred preserves.

"You're taking all of this with you," said Kagi. "I can't have supplies from supporters pile up too much, or the other boarders here might grow suspicious. Everything needs to keep moving from the railroad depot down to the Kennedy Farm."

Albert's eyes turned quizzical. Kagi added, "There's a little covered wagon out back and a horse for you to use."

Albert looked out the bedroom window and saw the wagon. A horse was nibbling on a hay bale at its side. When he turned around, Kagi was already gone, his footsteps pattering down the stairs. Albert opened the window to let in a warm breeze, then fell onto the bed and into sleep.

***

It was dark when Albert woke up and crept down the stairs, quietly so he wouldn't wake Kagi or the other boarders. Mary was already in the kitchen boiling water for coffee and slicing bacon. He wondered if she'd ever gone to bed.

"Good morning, love," she said. "Sit down for some breakfast."

"Yes, ma'am," he said, pulling a chair from the table. She set a cup of coffee in front of him, then several minutes later brought a plate with bacon, eggs, and potatoes.

"I hope you find your peace, Albert," she said as she set it down.

"My piece of what?" he asked before shoveling some eggs into his mouth.

Mary smiled but didn't answer, leaving him feeling like he'd missed a joke.

When he was finished, he went to try to load the crates onto the wagon himself, but they were heavy, so he waited for Kagi to wake up and help him. By the time that had happened and he had the wagon on the road, the hot summer sun was high overhead, broiling him where he sat on the driver's bench.

IX

The wagon jostled as it lumbered over tree roots and crawled around the boulders that marred the route into the mountains. Wherever murky puddles had liquified the road into mud, Albert had to unload all of the heavy crates and boxes from the wagon by himself, assist the horse by pushing the wagon from behind, then walk the cargo around the puddle to reload it. After yet another incident of such toil, he'd rolled a cigarette to reward himself as he bounced along on the driver's bench. Just as he was about to strike a match to light it, he saw the farm that Kagi had described to him in Chambersburg. There was a two-acre field, half of it mowed clean and the other half thick with hay, surrounded on all sides by dense forest. At the center was a log cabin mounted on a stone foundation and topped with a gabled roof. A cow and two pigs mooed and grunted in a corral next to it. On the porch sat a man with long dark hair whom Albert didn't recognize.

He called in a thick Maine accent for Albert to identify himself, then, after Albert had yelled his name, claimed not to have heard of it.

"Ask John Brown if he's heard of me!" shouted Albert.

The man opened the front door and said something to someone inside, then closed the door again. He allowed Albert onto the property, then introduced himself as Francis Meriam.

When Albert opened the door to let himself in, he saw Aaron sitting at a table playing cards with the Coppoc brothers and three others whom he didn't recognize. The two who looked alike were introduced as William and Dauphin Thompson from North Elba, who were brothers-in-law of Watson Brown and who'd come down with him to join his father and brothers, Owen and Oliver, for the raid. The third was a young Black man named John Copeland, an Oberlin College student who'd come with his uncle, Lewis Leary. John Brown was leaning against a windowsill, reading a folded newspaper with one hand and sipping a mug of coffee with the other. His daughter, Annie, and his daughter-in-law, Martha, both still in their teens, were peeling potatoes at a counter next to the stove. They all stopped what they were doing to look at Albert.

"I will lift up mine eyes unto the hills," said John Brown with a grin, "from whence cometh my help."

"I 'cometh' from Chambersburg," said Albert. "There's some boxes for you on the wagon."

Brown laid a hand gently on his shoulder. "Well done. The Lord shall preserve thy going out and thy coming in from this time forth, and even for evermore."

He sent Barclay and Dauphin to unload the wagon. Albert took a seat in an empty chair next to Aaron, who was recounting one of his misadventures in Ohio along his tortuous journey from Iowa to Maryland. Then, Annie cried out, "She's coming!"

All of the young men began to scramble up a narrow stairway to the loft above.

"Us too," said Aaron.

As Albert poked his head though the open trapdoor, he saw more than a dozen men gathered, smoking and playing cards. Some of them he recognized from Kansas Territory, including Jeremiah Anderson and William Leeman. Aaron closed the hatch.

"It's Mrs. Huffmaster," he continued in a whisper. "She

52

rents a garden on the next farm over. She's always snooping around and probably saw your wagon."

Only John Brown, Annie, Martha, and her husband, Oliver Brown, remained downstairs.

The men in the loft fell silent when they heard Mrs. Huffmaster's footfalls on the steps leading up to the front door. As Martha greeted her there, they listened in the darkness.

"I saw some young men unloading that wagon out there," said Mrs. Huffmaster. "I thought you might be having a soiree. Thought maybe I could help."

"I appreciate you thinking me a young man," said Brown.

"I didn't see a fluffy gray beard on any of these fellas," she said slowly.

"Well, there's no soiree, Mrs. Huffmaster, sorry to say," said Martha. "Just furniture and preserves."

"What kind of furniture would fit in a crate that size?" asked Mrs. Huffmaster.

"A bookshelf," said Brown. "I have to assemble it myself."

"What kind of preserves?" she asked.

"I'm not sure exactly," answered Martha, her voice trembling. "Strawberry, I think. Maybe raspberry."

"I just love strawberry preserves, and my strawberry plants have been so skimpy this year," said Mrs. Huffmaster. "Do you think I could have a jar? I have the most wonderful tomatoes that I can bring over to you later."

"Oh, you don't have to do that," said Martha.

There was a moment of silence as everyone waited for Mrs. Huffmaster to drop the subject, which she refused to do. "Just a little jar for the children," she said. "It's been so long since they've tasted strawberry, I can't even remember. I just feel so terrible about it, like I'm failing as a m-"

"I'm sure we can spare a jar," interrupted Brown. "Oliver, would you please?"

"Yes, father."

Albert could hear the crates and boxes being moved around, then the thud of one being set heavily upon the table.

"Let me see what kinds you have," said Mrs. Huffmaster.

"If you'll stand back, Mrs. Huffmaster," said Oliver. "I can pry it open for you."

"Why are you all acting so squirrelly?" she asked. "It's only preserves."

Albert held his breath as he heard the taps and creaks of a box being pried open.

***

Though the birds were already loud enough to waken Albert, the sky was still dark when he climbed down from the loft one morning to find Aaron sitting at the kitchen table, writing a letter by candlelight, the sun ever delaying its arrival in those lazy days of August. Three newcomers, two former slaves named Shields Green and Dangerfield Newby and a free Black man from Canada named Osborne Anderson, were sitting on ammunition boxes under a window, drinking coffee and playing dominos on a crate of rifles in the candle's dim glow.

"I didn't think you had a home to write to," said Albert.

Aaron smiled. "You're right," he said. It was a letter to a girl in Ohio named Jennie Dunbar, with whom he claimed to have fallen in love during his layover there.

Albert felt that metallic core pushing against his heart and lungs again. His breathing suddenly felt labored. "What's it like to love somebody?" he asked.

"It's nice, Al. When you've got something to say, there's someone who listens. In her company, I feel solitude without a trace of loneliness. It makes you feel like you're tethered to something, like you're not some piece of flotsam drifting around in the currents."

"It seemed like everyone in Kansas was a fella," said Albert. "And Johnstown wasn't much better."

Aaron laughed. "You're still a young man, Al. You'll find someone."

One by one, the others began to make their way down the

54

ladder from the loft, and Albert felt tension as though there had just been a disagreement among them. He watched them for a moment, and when no one confronted him or Aaron, his worry turned to puzzlement.

"Where's Old Brown?" Charles Tidd, a Kansas veteran, asked Annie.

"He's in the garden picking onions for breakfast," she answered.

Tidd told her to fetch him, which she did.

As soon as the door closed behind Brown, Tidd stepped forward. "We demand to know the plan. We all voted, and we've decided that we're all leaving if you don't tell us what it is." He flashed a glance at Albert, who understood not to contradict him.

Brown scratched his beard and scanned the men's faces. "Very well," he said. "Ye shall know the truth, and the truth shall make you free."

They were going to seize the United States Armory and Arsenal at Harpers Ferry, he told them, and use it to arm a slave army recruited from the farms and plantations of eastern Virginia, which would march from there throughout the South, liberating slaves along the way.

The men erupted at the news. Albert didn't reveal that this is what Kagi had told him in Chambersburg, and tried to hide his surprise that the others hadn't known.

"That's a suicide mission, and you know it!" shouted Brown's son, Owen. "It's supposed to be a raid, just like at Little Osage. We go in, grab a bunch of guns and ammunition, then get the hell out of there."

"My brethren," pleaded the father, "be strong in the Lord and in the power of his might. Put on the whole armor of God, that ye may be able to stand against the wiles of the devil. For we wrestle not against flesh and blood, but against principalities, against powers, against the rulers of the darkness of this world, against spiritual wickedness in high places."

Though their outrage was dampened somewhat, the men remained unconvinced.

"Suppose it were a raid," John Brown continued, "what would we do with all of those guns once we've seized them? Bring them back here for storage? Action must be taken, or the land will forever remain plagued by wickedness."

Some of the men nodded and mumbled words that Albert couldn't make out, but which sounded agreeable enough. But others demanded assurances. "How do we know that the townsfolk won't overrun us right away?" asked one. Another asked where the U.S. Army's closest troops were garrisoned, and how long it would take them to arrive at Harpers Ferry once the attack had started.

All of the details had been worked out, Brown assured them, but instead of explaining the plan himself, he summoned an emergency meeting to be attended by all of the raid's participants, including Kagi, whom he'd appointed "Secretary of War," and John Cook, who was the group's spy, having come directly from Kansas Territory to live in the town and gather information for the entire previous year. Without anyone objecting to the meeting, and the group assuaged in the meantime, Brown left immediately to fetch Kagi from Chambersburg, using the horse and wagon that Albert had brought from there.

After most of the men had climbed back up to the loft, Aaron slid a sheet of paper across the table toward Albert. "Why don't you sit down and write a letter to my sister?" he said. "She's a nice girl. She can be your fiancée."

"Oh yeah? What's her name?" Albert asked as he pulled out a chair from the table and sat down.

"Sue Ellen."

Albert repeated her name to himself as he wrote it on the paper.

The days that followed were spent in a sweltering limbo. In the mornings, the windows were covered on the outside in dew, and by mid-day they were coated on the inside in condensation from the stewing men, such that they remained in a constant state of murky translucence. Mrs. Huffmaster had returned with her tomatoes the day after Brown had left, and had lingered for more than an hour talking to Martha about rumors of runaway slaves and search parties in the area, making the men reluctant to leave the loft's suffocating confines even after she'd left. Up there they grumbled about the uncertainty of their fate and tried to soothe their anxieties with card games and books.

Albert worked on his letter to Sue Ellen. He struggled with writing to a girl whom he'd never met. How could he know whether her eyes were green like the leaves in early spring, or blue like a cloudless Kansan sky? Did she have blonde hair that reflected shimmering golden sunlight, or was it as dark as a moonless night? He didn't feel comfortable asking Aaron. But, by the time he heard the clopping of hooves and grinding of wagon wheels on the driveway that signaled Brown's return, he felt that he'd written enough to send it.

Brown dispatched Stewart Taylor, a new recruit from Chicago, to fetch Cook from Harpers Ferry. When he returned with Cook early the next afternoon, the valley was covered in a dark layer of clouds that concealed the sun and brushed the tops of the surrounding mountain ridges. As they were walking up the driveway, Brown saw them through a window and ordered Martha and Annie to deliver some vegetables from their garden to Mrs. Huffmaster and to keep her occupied for a few hours. The meeting was underway as soon as the two arrivals walked through the door.

"Without counsel, purposes are disappointed," Brown said to open the meeting, "but in the multitude of counsellors, they are established." Then, he yielded the floor to Cook.

Cook told the men about conversations he'd had with the people in town about their detest for slavery and their desire to see freedom for all men.

"But did you ask them how they'd like their town taken at gunpoint?" asked Tidd.

"We're not taking their town!" shouted Brown.

"I didn't," Cook replied. "But if they know that we're on the side of freedom, I have no doubt that they'll leave us to our work."

His words were received with folded arms and the shuffling of feet. Thunder rumbled overhead.

Kagi was invited to speak next, and he assured the men that they had supporters in all of the major Northern cities who were as wealthy as they were zealous, and who would pressure government officials to avoid a bloody confrontation. The risks simply were not as dire as the men feared, he explained.

The group began to discuss the matter, weighing what Cook and Kagi had said, and Albert felt the tension ease and believed that a resolution was within reach. Rain began to patter against the windows.

But then Brown spoke again. "I beseech you, brethren, by the name of our Lord Jesus Christ, that ye all speak the same thing, and that there be no divisions among you, but that ye be perfectly joined together in the same mind and in the same judgment." Then, he announced an ultimatum: If the men wouldn't accede to his plan, he would resign so they could elect another commander.

The room was thrown into a clamor as the men shouted at Brown and at each other. Albert felt his chest tighten as his mind raced back to his mother's farmhouse in Pennsylvania, the days spent drenched in sweat picking other men's crops, and the hard bed in a lonely guestroom.

"Order!" shouted Albert. The commotion stopped and the men all looked at him, most of them wearing puzzled expressions. Perhaps there was a compromise, he suggested, a way to mitigate the threat of an onslaught by federal troops without abandoning the goal of instigating a protracted slave rebellion.

"The nearest garrisons are to the east," offered Kagi. If the military were to respond to the attack, he explained, troops would have to cross one of the rivers, either the Potomac or the Shenandoah, which coursed along opposite sides of the town to its eastern point. If the raiders destroyed the two bridges there, they could stall the troops while they recruited their slave army in the Shenandoah Valley to the west.

Wind rattled the windows as a snare-drum roll of raindrops

beat against them. The young men, all twenty-one of them, watched Old Brown, waiting for his response. And young they were, with Owen and Dangerfield being the only two over thirty, and both of them more than fifteen years younger than their leader. Albert was holding his breath.

Brown exhaled deeply, then spoke. "And the multitude of them that believed were of one heart and of one soul," he said. He agreed to destroy the bridges.

The men roared in approval, whooping and hollering and slapping their knees and each other's backs. The sky was so dark that Albert couldn't tell whether it was day or night. Thunder rumbled over the valley and lightning webbed across the clouds. It would be a long time yet before the girls returned. Aaron stripped off his clothes and ran outside. Albert did likewise and so did the rest of them, even Old Brown. They jumped in puddles and slid across the grass as rainwater washed away the stink and grime from all of those days hidden in the loft, their wet, naked bodies shimmering under flashes of light.

Albert jumped as a streak of lightning split a tree at the edge of the hay field with a booming crack.

"Back inside!" shouted Brown, his eyes wide in alarm. The naked band of young men followed their leader in a herky-jerky run back to the porch, dancing on tiptoes to avoid sticks and rocks.

***

Patches of light blue broke through dark gray clouds, leaving Albert and the others guessing as to whether their last day at the Kennedy Farm would be spent drenched in rain. The men had relaxed their vigilance for Mrs. Huffmaster, as they would be gone before authorities could investigate the farm even if she did report them, and Albert was able to eat his breakfast of eggs and potatoes on the front porch. Just as the air was filling with the earthy dankness of a storm about to erupt, a ray of sun broke through the clouds to indicate

59

otherwise. Albert watched its light fall on the black and gray lightning-struck tree that prominently stood dead at the edge of the field.

It was a Sunday, so Brown gathered everyone together late in the morning for a prayer service in front of the cabin.

"My brethren," he began, "when thou goest out to battle against thine enemies, and seest horses, and chariots, and a people more than thou, be not afraid of them. For the Lord thy God is with thee, which brought thee up out of the land of Egypt. Hear, O Israel, ye approach this day unto battle against your enemies. Let not your hearts faint, fear not, and do not tremble. Neither be ye terrified because of them." He opened his eyes wide and bellowed, "For the Lord your God is he that goeth with you, to fight for you against your enemies, to save you!"

Then, he told them that they would be swearing another loyalty oath that morning, this time to the ideals that he'd written while a guest at Frederick Douglas's house in January of 1858, and which had been adopted as a "constitution" several months later at a meeting of abolitionists in Chatham, Ontario. Aaron was ordered to read this "Chatham Constitution" for Albert and the others of the group who'd never heard of it before.

Aaron stood atop a chair and unfurled the document like a scroll. "Whereas slavery, throughout its entire existence in the United States," he read, almost at a shout, "is none other than a most barbarous, unprovoked, and unjustifiable war of one portion of its citizens upon another portion, the only conditions of which are perpetual imprisonment and hopeless servitude or absolute extermination, in utter disregard and violation of those eternal and self-evident truths set forth in our Declaration of Independence."

He paused. Albert and some of the others clapped in encouragement; a few even cheered. Then, he read the articles. Aside from a provision allowing for the confiscation of all property from anyone caught holding slaves, Albert imagined that it didn't differ much from the constitution that the United

States already had. When Aaron was finished, he rolled the paper back up and handed it to Brown.

"Do you swear," Brown asked his men, holding his Chatham Constitution like a club, "to abide by and support this provisional constitution and these ordinances, so help you God?"

"I swear," mumbled Albert in unison with the others.

Brown told them to bow their heads. "Stand fast therefore in the liberty wherewith Christ hath made us free," he said, "and let us be not entangled again with the yoke of bondage. Blessed are we who hunger and thirst after righteousness, for we shall be filled. Amen."

"Amen," echoed the men.

With the service adjourned, Albert sat at the kitchen table with a sheet of paper, a pen, and a little jar of ink and spent the next several hours writing another letter to Sue Ellen. He hoped that it wouldn't be the last, he wrote. They'd exchanged several letters by then, and Albert felt that he now knew her well enough to capture her essence. He could imagine the way she flitted around her family's farm in Connecticut like a hummingbird in May, or how she focused on her sewing like a cat after a mouse, and he filled pages expressing his thirst to see her this way in person.

It was afternoon and the sky had turned completely overcast when Albert felt a tap on his shoulder that broke his focus and brought him back to reality. They were being gathered for a final meeting, and Albert went outside to congregate with the rest of the group in a semi-circle before Brown.

Three of them would be staying behind, Brown told them, to resupply the others at an appropriate time. They were the three men in the weakest condition for fighting: Owen Brown, whose right arm had been chronically injured since he was a boy, Francis Meriam, and Barclay Coppoc. Charles Tidd and John Cook would advance ahead of the others to cut the telegraph lines into town. Kagi and Aaron, following close behind, would then capture the night watchman on the

61

Baltimore & Ohio Railroad Bridge. The rest of them would follow with Brown and the wagon, crossing the bridge into Harpers Ferry. The next morning, a contingent would be sent from Harpers Ferry to collect the remaining weapons from the farm and move them to a schoolhouse tucked into a ravine just across the Potomac River from the town.

The men were dismissed without further ceremony, and Albert went back inside to sit with his letter. But with the raid now imminent, his daydreams of Sue Ellen were replaced with swirling memories of his gunfights in Kansas Territory: someone gutshot, writhing and howling in the dirt next to him; Albert's eyes choked with gun smoke as he strained to see who was shooting at them; a cacophony of voices shouting conflicting orders at each other. He considered the possibility that he may never meet Sue Ellen, and felt dread and doubt creeping into his imagination, spoiling his memories of those victories at Fort Scott and the Little Osage that had once served as his inspiration and reassurance.

By the time the sun had set too low for him to see well enough to write, he'd added nothing more to his letter. So, he signed what little he had, then walked out to the porch to watch the sun fall below the treetops behind the dead gray lightning-struck tree. Barclay was sitting on a rocking chair, smoking his pipe.

"Can you mail this for me?" Albert asked, handing him the letter without waiting for a response.

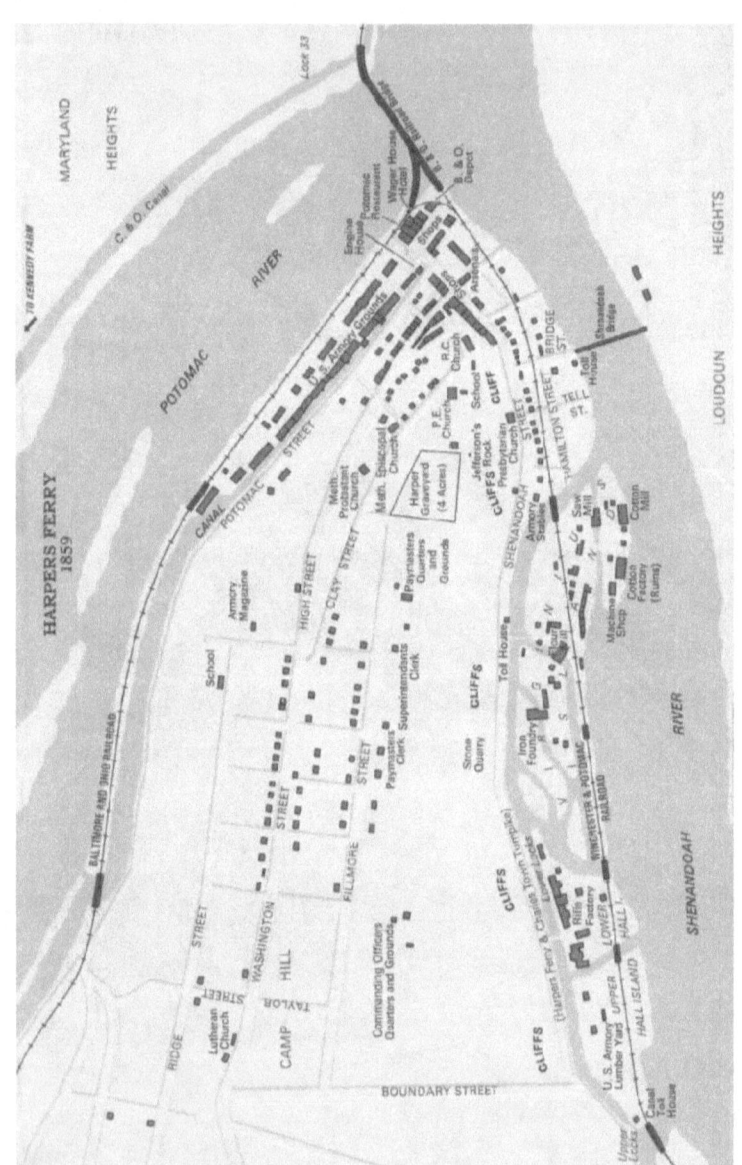

X

At eight o'clock, the men formed two marching columns behind their supply wagon. Thick raindrops pelted their ponchos and wide-brimmed hats. They would be marching in total darkness, under a moon obscured by clouds. Brown sat atop the driver's bench with a canvas tarp pulled tightly over his shoulders, the sleek breathing lump reminding Albert of a bullfrog waiting for a fly. Nobody was talking.

Even with the rain, Albert had wished that the march to the bridge would've taken longer. But it felt to him, with his mind racing to sort out contingencies and escape routes, that only a moment had passed before he spotted the town from a promontory alongside the road. In the night, the white clapboard houses set amongst dense trees looked like mushrooms growing in a bed of moss. Most of them still had at least one window illuminated by a lamp or fireplace. Streaks of white accented the black rivers on either side of the town as the water churned over shallow rocks on its way to meet at the confluence. At the end of town, just before the point where the two rivers met, was the massive, covered railroad bridge where they would cross into Virginia. At the other side, the tracks immediately split, with one line running southwest along

65

the Shenandoah River, and the other running northwest along the Potomac River and through the grounds of the United States Armory, a massive complex of warehouses and machine shops that appeared far larger in reality than Albert had imagined when looking at little rectangles on a map.

It was shortly after ten o'clock when the group passed the schoolhouse where the weapons would be brought. Several minutes later, they reached the bridge entrance, each one of them soaking wet and covered in mud. Aaron and Kagi had extinguished the lamps there and were waiting for the others as planned, which gave Albert some encouragement that the rest of the mission would proceed just as orderly.

Brown ordered Aaron and Kagi to walk across the bridge first, to scout for guards. As he watched them cross, Albert saw a lantern ignite ahead of them at the other end of the tunnel, bobbing closer as though someone were walking toward them with it in hand. Suddenly, the floating light fell to the platform with a clank and went dark, and the tunnel filled with the grunts and shouts of men grappling with one another. The bridge watchman became their first hostage.

Brown sent the rest of his men across. The sound of the water flowing beneath them drowned out their footsteps and the creaking of the wagon. When they reached the other side, he told his son, Watson, and Stewart Taylor to stand watch and to prevent anyone from entering from Maryland. Camp Hill sloped high above them, and the windows in the houses that lined the switchback road carved on its face now felt ominous to Albert, their peaceful glows having all been extinguished and replaced with guarded voids.

At the end of the short lane where they stood, called Potomac Street and lined with shops on either side, was the iron gate to the United States Armory complex. They walked over to it, then Aaron knelt in front and began to pry at the lock with a crowbar. As the clatter of his work interrupted the river's steady murmur, a guard emerged from the gatehouse.

John Cook pointed his rifle at him. "Open the gate," he said in a loud whisper.

Sheilds Green and William Leeman each grabbed one of the guard's arms and pinned him to the gate while Cook rummaged through his pockets for the key.

There was a loud clank as the padlock gave way. "I got it," said Aaron.

Brown drove the wagon through the open gate and parked it next to a red-brick fire-engine house directly inside. The bridge watchman and gatehouse guard were then escorted into the engine house, and their hands were tied behind their backs.

Brown announced to them that they were prisoners of war. "I came here from Kansas, and this is a slave state," he said. "I want to free all of the Negroes in this state. I have possession of the United States Armory, and if the citizens interfere with me, I must only burn the town and have blood."

Brown sent his other son, Oliver, and William Thompson to capture the bridge that crossed the Shenandoah River into the south of town. Meanwhile, he would lead a group to seize the United States Arsenal, which was a separate building across the street from the gate to the armory, and Hall's Rifle Works, a gun factory that was situated a half mile up the Shenandoah.

***

John Brown's contingent crept in the shadows between the streetlamps down Potomac Street to the arsenal's front gate. The rain had slowed to a drizzle, and only the rushing water of the rivers could be heard. Albert had his rifle cocked. Kagi had warned them that there would likely be an armed guard there, too, as it was where all of the guns were stored after they'd been manufactured at the armory. But there wasn't. Edwin Coppoc pried open the padlock with a crowbar and they walked right into the yard.

Kagi, Lewis Leary, and John Copeland inspected the small outbuilding to the right of the gate, while Brown, Albert, and the others proceeded to the long brick building at the center of the grassy lawn.

Edwin pried open the lock on the front door. The inside

67

was almost completely dark, illuminated only by the streetlamps far behind them and barely bright enough to see the stacks of crates inside.

"Hello!" Brown called out. "I have an urgent message from the telegraph office!"

They waited for a moment, then, after hearing only silence, went inside. Once sure that the building was empty of guards, Brown ordered Albert and Edwin to stay and guard it until further notice. Then, he left with Kagi and the others to capture Hall's Rifle Works.

Albert and Edwin climbed to the second floor and crouched at a pair of windows that overlooked the intersection of Potomac and Shenandoah Streets and the armory gate thereacross. They watched as several townsmen, stumbling home from the bars along Potomac Street back up to their houses on Camp Hill, were intercepted by the men posted at the armory gate and led to the engine house as prisoners. The captives' howls of protest echoed against the brick walls of the buildings, breaking the still of the night. Then, Albert and Edwin watched as Brown returned from the gun factory with Dauphin Thompson and Jeremiah Anderson and went back to the armory, its gate clanking behind them.

At midnight, Albert saw the group's wagon pull out from the armory gate with Aaron and Cook sitting on the driver's bench, and Tidd, Green, and Osborne Anderson walking beside it. The men on foot were armed with long pikes, their wet blades glinting in the light of the streetlamps. Slowly the wagon rolled through the mud of Shenandoah Street southwest toward the farms of the Shenandoah Valley, where they would recruit their slave army. Albert felt a rush of excitement as the insurrection appeared to be going exactly as Brown had planned. All that they had to do now was wait for the reinforcements to arrive.

Suddenly, the crack of a gunshot reverberated from the direction of the train tunnel and throughout the valley. Albert and Edwin shuffled over to a window on the northeast side to see what had happened, but their view was blocked by the

68

buildings across Potomac Street. They waited for another gunshot, but none sounded.

An hour and a half later, they heard the shriek of a locomotive's brakes resound from the same place, as an eastbound train rolled to a stop before the bridge. Albert craned his neck as though it would help him see over the rooftops that stood in his way. Then, another gunshot, followed almost immediately by panicked shouting.

Albert scrambled back to the window overlooking the armory to see if anyone was being sent out to respond to the shooting. After several minutes, he saw nobody emerge from the gate and heard no more gunfire. He guessed that both gunshots had been warnings issued by Watson Brown and Stewart Taylor, who were still guarding the bridge.

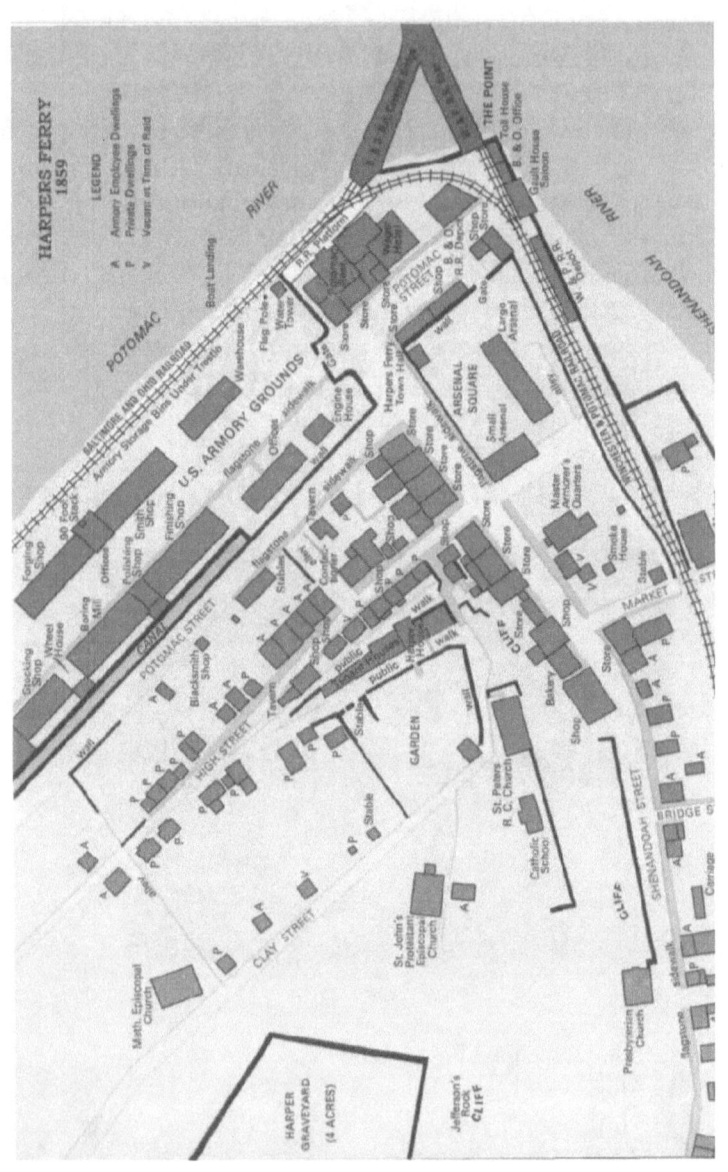

70

XI

The chirping of birds had begun to accompany the babbling of the rivers, and the sky behind the eastern ridgeline was brightening with dawn's approach. Mist rose from the water, veiling the red and yellow trees in a soft white haze.

A burly man marched down Potomac Street directly toward the front gate of the arsenal with a shotgun clutched in his hands. Albert raised his rifle to the windowsill and rested his finger on the trigger. He was deciding whether he would first yell out a warning when the man turned left on Shenandoah Street toward the gate of the armory.

The burly man raised his shotgun and fired a blast at Dangerfield and Jeremiah, who were standing just inside the armory gate, narrowly missing them both. Dangerfield raised his rifle to his shoulder and shot back. Their assailant yelped, then dropped his shotgun and collapsed into the mud. He lay there for a moment, then, using his gun as a crutch, stood himself on his good leg and hobbled into a nearby shop. A prosecutor would later tell Albert that the man, a grocery-store owner named Thomas Boerly, had bled to death almost immediately after collapsing onto the floor there.

Albert felt his excitement curdle into fear as he stuck his

71

head out the window and scanned down Shenandoah Street for any sign of Aaron or their reinforcements.

***

The sun had risen over the mountains when Albert heard the ringing of church bells from Camp Hill. Townspeople began to emerge from their houses and scurried, frantic, along the switchback lanes of their hillside village. Finally, he saw Aaron. He was driving a new four-horse wagon, with Cook driving the old wagon behind him. Walking alongside them were the militiamen who'd gone with them and about a dozen Black recruits. Albert wondered at their small number, but soothed himself with thoughts of a larger group of reinforcements not far behind.

He watched Osborne arm the recruits with pikes and guns, then saw about half of them climb onto the back of the new wagon with Tidd and Leeman while Cook mounted the driver's bench. As Cook drove them across the covered bridge to Maryland and the Kennedy Farm, Albert couldn't understand why they were leaving to resupply when they'd already captured nearly all of the guns in Harpers Ferry. But that had been the plan from the start. A long gray cloud floated over the armory complex as the train that had been stopped by the bridge was allowed to continue its journey east.

Edwin left his position and went down to stand at the arsenal gate, where he told workers arriving for their morning shift that the building was closed and directed them to the armory. Albert watched as they went to where they'd been told and, along with the workers who were reporting for work at the armory, were taken prisoner and led to the engine house. He counted more than seventy of them.

A gunshot echoed from the hillside, then another, as townspeople began to fire on the engine house and the armory from higher ground, muzzles flashing in the windows of the houses there. A man stepped onto the wooden sidewalk in front of one of the shops on Potomac Street, drew a revolver

72

from his hip, and fired a shot at Edwin. The bullet narrowly missed, glancing off the stone wall next to his head with a ping and a little puff of dust. Albert raised his rifle to the windowsill, found the gunman in his sight, and pulled the trigger.

The target dropped his revolver and grabbed his leg. An elderly Black recruit emerged from the armory gate with a shotgun. Albert watched him raise the gun to his shoulder and shout something at the wounded man. Then, a boom echoed throughout the valley, and the man clutched his chest and fell face first onto the sidewalk.

***

Dense fog over the Potomac blocked Albert's view of Maryland on the other side. The covered bridge penetrated the thick gray cloud like a pipeline from the abyss. The sun was high overhead, peeking through the overcast, when gunfire and shouting erupted from the blackness within. Albert hurried to the window, raised his rifle to the sill, and took aim at the tunnel exit.

When a group of armed townsmen ran out, a volley of rifle fire burst from the armory gate. Albert took a shot from the window, but was unable to see through the smoke whether he'd hit anyone. Once it had cleared, he saw that several of the attackers had fallen. Those who hadn't were dragging the wounded back to the bridge.

Then, Albert watched Brown run from the armory with a sword raised high over his head, leading his militiamen down Potomac Street toward him and Edwin at the arsenal. A thunderous volley of gunfire discharged from the windows of the shops on either side, and Dangerfield collapsed to the ground. Brown turned around and led a hasty retreat back to the armory. In the confusion, Edwin left to join him there, while Osborne ran to the arsenal. Albert called down to Osborne from a window, then ran down the stairs to meet him at the door.

Rain was falling in torrents when Albert saw William Thompson leave the armory gate escorting a hostage and holding a white flag of truce. Two armed townsmen walked out to meet him. Immediately, one of them ripped the flag from Thompson's hand and threw it to the ground, while the other fixed his rifle on him. The hostage fled down Shenandoah Street, and the townsmen escorted Thompson into one of the shops nearby. Claps of gunfire continued to resound from the hillside, followed by the pings of metal on stone from the engine house, just as they had ever since Dangerfield's death. Sometimes, Brown's men shot back.

Then, the armory gate opened again, and Aaron and Watson emerged leading another hostage down Potomac Street. They'd just passed behind a building that blocked Albert's view when he heard a burst of gunfire and saw a cloud of smoke rise from where they'd gone. Watson stumbled back toward the armory gate, clutching his stomach and using his rifle as a cane, but Aaron didn't reappear. Albert felt tears well in his eyes and run down his cheeks, uncertain of whether his closest friend was alive or dead.

Some townspeople had gathered around Dangerfield's body on the side of the road. With dirty knives, they hacked off his ears and fingers and took other macabre souvenirs from his corpse. Several of them shoved sticks into his wounds. Albert wanted to shoot, but the crowd's focus was entirely on the armory gate and the engine house, leaving him to wonder if they even knew that he and Osborne were there. Osborne was watching the scene unfold from another window, expressionless and silent, and Albert sensed that he had the same thought.

As the gunfire between the men at the engine house and the hillside snipers persisted, a crowd of nearly eighty armed townsmen had poured out from the covered bridge and were assembled at the tunnel exit, out of sight from Brown's men at the armory.

Osborne turned to Albert and spoke for the first time in hours. "We have to leave," he said.

XII

Albert followed Osborne as he scrambled down the stairs and to a window in the back of the building on the southeast side, facing the Shenandoah River. Osborne pushed open the shutters, revealing the high stone causeway that brought the Winchester & Potomac Railroad to its junction with the Baltimore & Ohio at the covered bridge.

"That's where we're going," said Osborne, pointing at the causeway. "We climb up there and run west to the gun factory with Kagi and them."

The pair climbed out the window and sprinted across the backyard to the causeway's stone retaining wall. After scaling it, they ran along the tracks away from the gunfire. The sky darkened further as the afternoon crept toward the evening. As rain continued to pour, the fog that rose from the river wafted across the causeway, obscuring the view ahead of them.

The dark silhouette of a man holding a rifle appeared on the tracks in the light gray mist. Startled, Albert and Osborn slowed their approach, unsure of whether he was one of their own, coming from the gun factory. Albert strained to make out the features of his face, but before he could do so, Osborne raised his rifle.

"Put the gun down," he ordered.

The man acquiesced. Albert glanced at his face as he went to grab the weapon and didn't recognize it.

"You're our prisoner now," said Osborne.

"You're making a big mistake," said the man. "You might as well let me go because you've got nowhere to take me. All your men at the Rifle Works are dead."

Albert felt a lump form in his throat as he found himself believing what he'd just heard. But if he and Osborne turned back now, they'd face certain capture; they at least had to investigate. "We'll just see about that," said Albert, swallowing his dread. Then, he spun their prisoner around and pushed him forward.

They walked further along the causeway, then continued where it ended and the tracks cut across the little islands that dotted the riverside. Gradually, the din of combat faded, and by the time they spotted the lamplit windows of the rifle factory glimmering through the fog ahead of them, they heard only the crunch of gravel under their boots and the gentle rippling of the Shenandoah River.

Albert and Osborne stopped. Their prisoner walked a few steps further, then turned around.

"I thought you wanted to see for yourselves?" he gloated. "So, let's go."

The man's nonchalance erased all of Albert's doubts. "We believe you," Albert said. "Did you kill any of them yourself?"

The smile dropped from the man's face, and he began to shake. "No, sir. Absolutely not." His voice was trembling.

"So, why do you have that gun?" asked Osborne.

"Everyone's got a gun. They called up the town militia when they – or y'all, I guess – attacked the armory. I grabbed my gun and ran out when they knocked on my door just like everyone else."

Albert knew that shooting him would likely alert someone to where they were. "I'll tell you what," he said. "We'll let you live if you promise not to tell anyone that you saw us."

Light returned to the man's eyes. "Oh yes," he said, nodding

78

his head vigorously. "Mum's the word." He mimed sewing his lips closed. "I ain't seen nothing."

They stood there for a moment, the man looking back and forth between Albert and Osborne.

"Well, get going," said Osborne.

"What about my gun?"

"We're keeping the gun," said Albert.

Their former prisoner brushed between them, bumping Albert's shoulder. Then he disappeared into the mist behind them, back toward the arsenal. Albert and Osborne were once again alone.

"Up the hill," said Osborne, pointing at the wooded cliffside along Shenandoah Street. "Let's go."

They ran through some trees to the canal that ran alongside the railroad.

"Don't make a splash," said Osborne.

They eased into the water, which was as deep as Albert's chest, and waded gently across, then climbed up the bank on the other side, ran across the road, and clambered up Camp Hill's southern face.

***

Albert and Osborne were huddled together for warmth in a thicket of brush, waiting for the dusk to darken into night so they could resume their escape, when they heard a shout from the road below them.

"They went this way!" It was their former prisoner. "Up the cliff!" he shouted.

Albert peeked through the bushes and saw armed townsmen gathering below them. "What do we do?" he whispered. He felt panic invading his consciousness, scrambling his thoughts.

When he turned to look at Osborne, he saw him with his rifle already aimed down the cliffside. Osborne pulled the trigger and a shot rang out. "I suggest you do the same," he said.

79

The men below started to yell at each other. A few moments later, gunfire erupted from the bottom of the hill, and bullets thwacked against the trees over Albert's and Osborne's heads. They returned fire. It was enough to keep any of their pursuers from daring to venture up the slope to their position. When the sky darkened into night several minutes later, the townsmen withdrew back toward the armory. Albert kept his gaze fixed on the street below, certain that they would return.

***

The temperature plummeted as Albert and Osborne continued their journey in the night. Soaked because of the unrelenting rain and having waded through the canal hours earlier, they shivered as they groped blindly for roots and trees, climbing their way to the hilltop. Their cold, wet clothes clung to their trembling bodies, constricting their movements. They had waited several hours after their skirmish with the townsmen before continuing their flight, and, when they finally reached the summit, only a few of the houses there still had lamps lit in the windows. Running through yards and gardens under the cover of darkness, they crossed through the neighborhood there to the cliffs on the northern side, then descended to the Potomac River. Albert could feel his wet feet starting to slough in his sodden boots, so he took them off and continued barefoot.

They ran westward along Potomac Street, away from town, until they saw a rowboat tied to the dock of a sawmill. They climbed in, and Albert untied the mooring rope and pushed them from the dock while Osborne set the oars in their locks. Then, with smooth, steady strokes, Osborne rowed them across the river to Maryland and, for a few minutes, Albert felt soothed by the murmur of raindrops falling into the water. Once on the other side, they followed the towpath of a canal seven miles up the Potomac until they saw the white brick lockhouse and sign that marked lock number thirty-seven. The Kennedy Farm was only a few hundred yards away.

Albert and Osborne rummaged through cupboards and drawers and broke open crates and barrels looking for something to eat. The three men who'd been left to guard the farm – Owen, Barclay, and Francis – had already fled, and it appeared that they'd taken all of the food with them.

"Let's try the schoolhouse," said Albert.

"There wasn't any food there in the first place," Osborne responded.

"Well, we can't stay here. We might as well check on our way to being gone."

Osborne didn't argue with him, and once again they were shivering and soaked in rain as they clawed their way along tree-covered hillsides, back toward Harpers Ferry.

When they spotted the schoolhouse, they snuck through the trees around its perimeter looking for guards. Once they felt certain that there was nobody watching the building, they approached the front door.

"Should I knock?" asked Albert.

Osborne pushed it open.

The room was stocked with crates of rifles and bundles of pikes. The desks were askew, and writing slates and chalk were strewn across the floor. There was no food to be found.

By the time they'd finished their search, the rain had stopped and the eastern sky was paling from its deep twilight blue.

"If we fall asleep in here, we might as well just go the jailhouse and ask for a cot," said Osborne.

Albert nodded, and they once again set off clambering along the steep wooded slopes of the river valley. When they reached a promontory with a view of the town, they huddled together under a tree and fell asleep.

***

Albert awoke to the sound of gunfire coming from the

81

valley below. On a boulder several feet away, Osborne was lying prone, watching the action. Albert climbed up to join him. A little cloud of smoke rose from where their confederates were shooting from the armory gates.

"It looks like they're trying to break out and come across the bridge," said Albert, referring to the covered bridge across the Potomac. Noticing that both of the bridges into town were still intact, he wondered if Old Brown had ever intended to honor his promise to destroy them. He'd placed their arsenal in a schoolhouse across the river, after all.

"We can provide cover fire from this side of the river," said Osborne. "Let's get closer to the bridge."

They crept along the hillside, hidden by thick brush. When they approached within a few hundred feet of the bridge entrance, they saw that it was guarded by federal troops.

"Let's get out of here," whispered Osborne as he brushed past Albert and scurried up the slope and away from Harpers Ferry. Albert would later be told that the gunshots that morning were from a last stand by Brown and the other men at the engine house against ninety federal marines led by Colonel Robert E. Lee and Lieutenant J.E.B. Stuart.

***

Albert and Osborne followed the top of the ridge until it ended, then ran a mile eastward across fields dotted with tall, brown shocks of harvested corn. They were headed to South Mountain, a long, forested ridge that extended north seventy miles into Pennsylvania, past Chambersburg and nearly all the way to Harrisburg. They had made it an entire day without being seen, and the rest of their escape appeared to be virtually guaranteed. But when the sun set, Albert found himself shivering wildly, as his stomach twisted itself in knots reminding him that he hadn't eaten in two days.

"I need to eat something," he said to Osborne, almost pleading.

Osborne said that he was hungry, too, and the two made

their way down the side of the mountain to a cornfield where they each plucked a half-dozen ears from a shock before darting back into the woods. Concealed by a ring of boulders high up the slope, they made a fire, roasted the corn, and ate half of it, saving the rest for the next day.

The second day of their flight proceeded in much the same way as the first until, just as the sun was setting, they descended into a ravine where there was a road winding along a creek through the mountains. Osborne suggested that they follow it to see if they could figure out where they were. Albert's feet stung from the cuts and blisters he'd accumulated while running barefoot along rocky, tree-covered mountainsides, but he wanted urgently to know whether they'd made it back across the Mason-Dixon Line. After walking several miles, they came to a sign at an intersection. "Gettysburg – 10 mi.," it said, with an arrow pointing east. They were in Pennsylvania.

Albert collapsed onto the ground and leaned his rifle on a rock. "I'm done," he said, too exhausted to walk another step. "You go on without me. I'll meet you at Mary Ritner's boarding house." Sensing Osborne hesitate, he added, "It'll be safer if we separate now, anyway."

Osborne nodded, then helped Albert to his feet for a parting embrace. As Osborne took him in his arms, Albert began to sob, overwhelmed by the idea of having to survive on the run alone.

"You'll be alright," said Osborne, patting him on the back. Then, Osborne disappeared into the trees, leaves rustling and branches waving slightly behind him. Albert would never see him again.

XIII

It was dark when Albert woke up, lying in a pile of leaves not far from where Osborne had left him on the side of the road. Then, after another night spent trudging along South Mountain, much more slowly now that he no longer felt pressure to keep pace with Osborne, he finally arrived at the Chambersburg Turnpike. He turned west to follow the road into Chambersburg and, as the sun was rising, reached the railroad tracks that marked the town's edge. To avoid being spotted by someone on the street, he kept hidden in the brush along the tracks as he made his way to the train depot behind the Ritner Boarding House.

At the depot lot, the railway terminated, splitting into several sidetracks that meandered between workshops and sheds. A few of them led to the three bays of an enormous brick train shed, where there were three giant, black locomotives, one in each. Two of them were dormant, while the third was discharging a jet of black smoke from its chimney, ready to depart. Metallic clanks of iron tools and brawny shouts from mechanics reverberated throughout the complex, echoing off the walls of its several buildings. Opposite the railyard from the train shed, a line of boxcars was parked next to a long loading dock, detached from any engine. Albert snuck alongside it as he crossed the property, to stay hidden from the workmen.

At the depot's south side was a meadow that separated it from the Ritner Boarding House. Albert crawled through the tall grass to the white picket fence that marked the edge of Mary's backyard. Peering between the slats, he saw no movement in the windows, nor any guards posted at the back door. He opened the gate gently, then crept across the lawn to the back porch. There, he peeked through the kitchen window and saw Mary cooking at the stove. With a big smile, he tapped on the glass eagerly, hopeful that he was about to eat a hot meal.

Mary turned to the noise, and when her eyes met his, they widened in fear. She shook her head quickly. Then, a soldier emerged from the hallway behind her. Albert dropped his rifle as he turned and ran back across the yard, out the gate, and through the tall grass toward the train depot. From there, he followed the railroad tracks northeast toward Harrisburg.

Several minutes later, a train whistle blared behind him and, for the first time since he'd started running, he turned around. The active locomotive had left the shed and had been connected with the boxcars, and the train had just left the depot. Behind it, the soldier was jogging after him.

As the train passed, Albert grabbed a hold of a little iron ladder affixed to the side of one of the boxcars and hoisted himself onto a small platform at its end. He poked his head out and looked back at the soldier, who'd already turned around to begin his slow walk back to the house. Albert watched him for a moment, letting the wind tousle his hair, until he was interrupted by pangs in his stomach. His roasted ears of corn long gone, he curled into a ball on the platform and tried to sleep through the pain.

XIV

Albert was awakened by the train's whistle signaling their arrival in Carlisle, where the tracks ran through the center of town. Wooden sidewalks on either side were crowded with pedestrians bustling between the shops, and horses and carts clogged the streets. The train's brakes screeched as it came to a stop. Albert felt panic replace the pain of starvation as he realized that if people were looking for him, he'd be spotted quickly. He looked out from between the cars and saw railyard workers walking along each side, inspecting the gaps. Waiting for the train to start moving again wasn't an option.

He'd hoped to slip away unnoticed, but when he jumped down from the platform, he bumped right into one of the workmen, who immediately grabbed his collar.

"I've got one!" he shouted to his coworker, who came scrambling from the other side of the train, leaping over a hitch between two cars.

"You look like hell, even for a stowaway" he continued, looking at Albert. "What's your name?"

"William Harrison," said Albert.

"The hell it is," said the coworker. "That's the name of that president who died a few years ago after a month in office."

He squinted his eyes and narrowed his gaze. "Are you one of them boys running from Harpers Ferry?"

Albert regretted not having given thought to an alias beforehand. He considered running, but by then the commotion had captured the attention of several onlookers.

"I'll fetch the sheriff," said an elderly gentleman before shuffling off.

Albert was stuck with being "William Harrison."

***

It had been so long since Albert had eaten regular meals of any kind or had a quiet place to sleep for the night that the first few days in jail felt like a relief. But when one morning he asked a guard for a cup of coffee and his request was met with laughter, he realized the weight of his predicament. The nights began to feel colder, he now smelled mildew on his blanket, and he noticed spots of mold on the bread that they gave him twice daily.

A group of lawyers arrived one day to tell him that they'd been hired to defend him. When he asked them who was paying for their services, one of them told him that unnamed "benefactors" had agreed to cover their fee. They then went on to explain that the Governor of Virginia had requested his extradition, so he could be tried with the other raiders who'd been arrested.

"But I'm not one of the raiders," said Albert. "I'm William Harrison."

He detected smiles flash beneath the lawyers' serious expressions. "Yes, of course," said one of them. "We'll make sure that your story gets told."

***

Albert had expected there to be spectators, having sat through the trial in New York, but when the sheriff's deputy led him into the courtroom in Carlisle, he was shocked to see the gallery packed with people standing shoulder-to-shoulder, craning their necks to catch a glimpse of him.

"You're famous," said the deputy wryly, before leaving him at the defendant's table with his attorneys. His hands were kept bound in cuffs behind him.

The judge banged his gavel to mark the start of the hearing. "The court has been convened on a petition of habeas corpus filed by the Governor of Virginia," he declared, "for the extradition of Albert Hazlett to Jefferson County, where Harpers Ferry is located, to face trial with the other conspirators who have been apprehended after the attack there."

Then, the attorney for the State of Virginia called witnesses from the raid one by one, and each one of them pointed a finger at Albert while testifying that they'd seen him during the attack. One of them even testified that he'd seen Albert kill the man who'd shot at Edwin. But on cross-examination, they all admitted that they had no personal knowledge of his real name. Albert's lawyers argued vehemently that he couldn't be extradited unless the State of Virginia proved that he was actually Albert Hazlett, and not "William Harrison."

After the evidence had been presented, the judge announced that he was ready to make a ruling. He began, "We are already of the opinion that the requisition presented to us is legally and formally right, but there is no evidence that we have any man in our custody named Albert Hazlett, whom we can deliver on the requisition."

Albert felt a flash of hope upon hearing these words.

But it was swiftly dashed, as the judge continued, "But we are satisfied that a monstrous crime has been committed. That the prisoner was there and participated in it has been clearly testified to by three witnesses. We will, therefore, recommit him to await the requisition of the Governor of Virginia."

"We're sorry, Albert," said one of his lawyers.

Then, two deputies grabbed him by the arms and led him back to the jail.

XV

The gas lamps trembled as cold November air blew through the barred windows of the Charles Town jail. A brass band was playing a polka outside for the revelers who'd gathered for the trial of John Brown, which had begun several days before Albert had arrived from Pennsylvania.

Albert listened to the drums and bootstomps of a platoon marching back and forth in front of the jail as he waited for Aaron, who was lying on a cot across the cell, to wake up. Albert was curled up on his own cot, trying to still his shivering body after having draped his only blanket over his sleeping friend. The other cells on the block were occupied by their confederates from Brown's militia: Shields Green and John Copeland were in one cell, Edwin Coppoc and John Cook in another, and both with a guard seated by the door.

He'd been shocked when the guards had led him to a cell with his best friend, but as soon as Aaron woke up, he understood why.

"Albert?" said Aaron in wide-eyed surprise.

Albert cast a glance at the guard standing nearby and saw him smiling widely. "William Harrison" had been exposed.

He turned his attention back to his friend. "I thought you

were dead," he said. "I saw you get shot."

"Shot, but not dead," said Aaron. "Just halfway there." He explained how he'd been shot six times, and how a hostage had been released from the engine house to pull him into a nearby hotel, where a doctor had dressed his wounds. "Saved my life just long enough for them to kill me again."

There was a knock on the door to the cellblock, and a guard opened the small peephole door to talk to whomever was on the other side. Then, he turned around with a beaming smile. "Death by hanging!" he proclaimed. Brown had been sentenced. The execution was scheduled for December 2, 1859.

For the first time since his arrest in Carlisle, Albert felt entirely hopeless. "I don't want to die, Aaron," he whimpered.

"I know you don't, Al."

"So, what do I do?"

"You should pray." Then, he pulled a blanket from on top of himself and flung it at Albert. "And take your blanket back. I don't need it any more than you do."

***

White fluffy snow fell gently outside the window of their cell as they opened several packages that had been sent to them by abolitionist admirers for Christmas. Most of the gifts were confiscated by the guards, but the pair were allowed to keep several items of warm clothes, as well as some jam, crackers, and cheese. A wealthy Quaker abolitionist from New Jersey named Rebecca Spring, who'd met Aaron when visiting Brown after his capture, had even sent them each a new pair of shoes. Albert couldn't remember the last time his toes hadn't felt wet, numb, or sore.

Brown had been executed a few weeks earlier, on December 2nd as scheduled, and the other four confederates who'd been in jail with them had been executed on December 14th. With each event, Albert and Aaron fell into deeper quiet, speaking less and less, and focusing their attention on their letters. They would be tried together in February, when the court resumed for its spring session. Albert's trial had been delayed by the habeas corpus proceeding in Pennsylvania, and Aaron's case had been paused when a federal prosecutor, who envisioned a grand conspiracy involving Republican politicians, made an unsuccessful attempt to remove his case to federal court.

Aaron wrote to his fiancée, Jennie Dunbar, nearly every day. Albert tried to do the same for Sue Ellen, but he found it impossible, after the executions of Brown and the others, to imagine a future for himself other than hanging from a scaffold in front of a crowd of spectators.

"What are you even writing to Jennie?" he asked Aaron, in search of ideas. But it was only the same romantic sentiments that no longer felt real to Albert now that marriage and a family were so resolutely beyond reach.

He had written letters, meanwhile, to his brothers and mother, to tell them where he was and how he'd arrived there. Feeling their disapproval sharply, he'd labored to explain how the raid on Harpers Ferry served a noble purpose, and that it hadn't been another selfish act, like stealing from his employer or horse theft. But no response ever came, and he wasn't inspired to try again for one on that Christmas morning.

"I'm sorry, Sue Ellen," he wrote at last. There would be no wedding, and no little farm with cows and cornfields. There would be no holiday meals with Aaron and Jennie, and no clutch of children playing at their feet. "I ask only that you pray for me, too, when you're praying for Aaron." She didn't write back.

***

When the court reconvened in February for Albert's and Aaron's trial, there was no more revery or brass bands, and only a few dozen soldiers were stationed around the courthouse. Inside the courtroom, the gallery was once again filled with spectators, but the enthusiasm of the prior autumn had vanished with the leaves. Wrapped in coats and scarves,

93

they wore the bored expressions of an audience watching a play that they'd seen just the weekend before, already aware of its ending and itching to get there.

There were no surprises. The same witnesses were called, each of whom gave the same testimony as they had during the trials of Brown and the other conspirators. The prosecutor didn't even bother to call Albert's jailhouse guard to the stand, who could've provided his real name. Like at the hearing in Pennsylvania, a witness again claimed to have seen Albert shoot and kill the man who'd shot at Edwin. As far as Albert was concerned, that had been an act of self-defense. But his lawyers didn't dare put him on the stand to argue the point.

Albert and Aaron were sentenced together on Valentine's Day. Albert's attorneys made a final argument that the prosecution had never established definitively that his name was "Albert Hazlett," and not "William Harrison," but the judge rejected it swiftly. Twenty federal soldiers stood behind them in case they tried to run. Each of the condemned was allowed to make a final statement.

Aaron rose slowly to speak first, holding onto the side of the defendant's table as he wobbled under fatigue from his wounds. He began by pointing out some falsities in the testimony given against him by several of the witnesses, then thanked his attorney, guards, and physician. "When I think of my brothers slaughtered and sisters outraged in Kansas," he said in conclusion, "my conscience does not reprove me for my actions. I shall meet my fate manfully."

Albert spoke next. Like Aaron, he used the opportunity to point out errors in the witnesses' testimony against him. "But I forgive them all," he said. He also thanked the guards and his attorneys, who, he said, had "done more on my behalf than Northern counsel could have done." At the end, he said, "I am innocent of murder, but am prepared to meet my fate."

The judge sentenced them to hang publicly on Friday, March 16, 1860.

**

When they got back to their cell and the barred iron door slammed behind them, Albert sat on his cot and asked Aaron, "Why do they make us wait a month? Why don't they just kill us now?"

"So we can get our affairs in order."

"I don't have any affairs to get in order," said Albert. "Maybe if I tell them that, they'll just put a bullet in my head tonight." He tried to smile for Aaron, to show him that it had been a joke, but a well of tears pushed its way upward and he began to sob violently.

Aaron sat down next to him and put an arm around his shoulders. "You have affairs, Al," he said. "You need to tell your family what's happened."

Albert nodded slightly, finding himself unable to speak.

XVI

"We're all so proud of you."

"Thank you, Mrs. Spring," said Albert. As he watched the woman sitting in a chair across the cell from him and listened to her kind words, he could only think about his mother, finding himself unexpectedly surprised by her absence on this final day of his life on earth.

"Eternal life shall be yours," she said. "And as for the end of your–" she daubed her eyes with a handkerchief, choking up. "I've taken care of the arrangements for your burial. You won't be forgotten, Albert."

She paused for a moment. Albert watched her, thinking that she was searching for the right words. But when he saw her shoulders begin to heave gently, he realized that she couldn't speak through her sobbing. "It's alright, Mrs. Spring," he said.

"No, it's not alright! This is all so unfair!" She began to shake her head but, unable to say another word, offered no resistance as the guards gently guided her from her chair and out of the cell. Beyond the threshold, she turned to look at him.

"Thank you for coming," he said as the heavy metal door swung closed behind her.

97

Albert got up and stood at the door to look through its bars into the cell across the hall, where Aaron was meeting with Jennie Dunbar. There, he could see her tear-stained cheeks, their long embraces sprinkled with kisses, and their tense lips speaking serious words.

A guard stepped into his view. "Back up," he said. Albert had another visitor.

Albert sat back down on his cot and watched, somewhat startled, as his brother Jonas entered.

"I'm here on behalf of the family, Al," he said. "We're sorry to see you in this state. They've asked me to give you their condolences and goodbyes and, of course, I do the same."

"Mom couldn't come?"

"The family wants you to make a full confession. Her too."

"I didn't murder anyone, Jonas. We were being shot at."

"I'm sorry you see it that way. Farewell, Absalom."

"How could I possibly fare well?"

"Goodbye, then."

***

When it was time to go to the gallows, Albert and Aaron were seated side by side on the back of a wagon, their shoulders brushing gently against one another as the horses pulled them slowly toward the outskirts of town. Clouds raced across the sky as a cold wind lashed Albert's face. His mind returned to that gap in South Mountain where he'd parted with Osborne, the only one from Brown's militia – other than the three who'd remained at the Kennedy Farm – who'd managed to escape with his life. He imagined an alternative future where he'd kept going and had married Sue Ellen and they'd raised cattle on a farm in Kansas Territory surrounded by their children.

He was torn from this final daydream by the guards grabbing his arms and pulling him from the wagon. The wooden framework of the gallows towered above him. As he plodded slowly up the long staircase to the platform, his legs felt leaden. A line of federal troops stood between him and a crowd of spectators bundled in heavy woolen cloaks. Some of them cursed and jeered him, but the majority looked on with blank expressions, as though they were simply curious to see how he'd hang.

He and Aaron were positioned over a pair of trapdoors at the center of the platform. Aaron leaned over and firmly kissed Albert on the lips. "I love you," he said. "We'll be together again soon."

Albert could only nod his head.

While two deputies placed nooses around Aaron's and Albert's necks, the sheriff read out the court's order to the crowd. They were about to witness "the execution of Aaron Dwight Stevens and William Harrison," he told them, Albert's true identity having never been established at his trial. As a burlap sack was pulled over Albert's head, he stared ahead in wide-eyed terror at the bright orb of light where the sun shined through. Then, he heard a click and felt a sudden drop as the trapdoor swung open beneath him.

EPILOGUE

In the summer of 1899, an artist named Katherine McClellan was at work in her photography studio in Saranac Lake, New York, when she received a letter from a civil servant in Washington, D.C., named Dr. Thomas Featherstonhaugh. A self-described John Brown enthusiast and collector of memorabilia from the raid, he had written to ask whether she would accept delivery of several corpses. He'd located the bodies of Oliver Brown, John Kagi, Lewis Leary, William Leeman, Dangerfield Newby, Stewart Taylor, and William and Dauphin Thompson in an unmarked mass grave along the banks of the Shenandoah River. It was his intention to reinter them with John Brown, who'd been buried at his farm in North Elba, with "some decent ceremonies to attend the burial that will make the matter memorable and historic."

Albert and Aaron would be included, too. Rebecca Spring had kept her promise to arrange their funeral, and they had been buried in a small cemetery on the grounds of the Raritan Bay Union, a utopian community that she and her husband had established on their estate in Perth Amboy, New Jersey. It had been a small service, having not been announced publicly to avoid drawing protestors, and had been attended only by a few of the community's members. The property had since been sold to a tile factory, Featherstonehaugh explained, that wanted to remove the cemetery so the factory could expand its operations. So, by a stroke of luck, their corpses would be available for the public reburial, as well.

Because McClellan had been the author and publisher of *A Hero's Grave in the Adirondacks*, a twenty-page illustrated pamphlet that was sold to tourists at John Brown's farm, Featherstonhaugh thought that she might be receptive of both the idea and the bodies. She was, and agreed to chair the committee that would organize the ceremony.

On August 30, 1899, a funeral procession carried a silver-handled casket, in which all of the remains had been packed together, under a military escort from the opera house in Lake Placid three miles to John Brown's farm. Hundreds were in attendance, as the event had been advertised throughout the country and had attracted tourists from near and far.

The service at the grave site began with everyone singing "Onward Christian Soldiers," followed by a prayer. Then came speeches from local clergymen and journalists, each of whom extolled the raiders' legacy as the spark that ignited the Civil War and incinerated the institution of slavery. After a preacher closed the ceremony with a benediction, everyone broke into an impromptu rendition of "John Brown's Body."

Absalom (Albert) Hazlett

1837-1860

This book is dedicated to
Brian McMenamin,
an old friend

ACKNOWLEDGMENTS

Foremost, I thank my wife, Amanda, for being supportive of my writing hobby, and for all of the hard work that she puts into proofreading and editing as the first reader of my manuscripts, including this one. She also drove me to Indiana, Pennsylvania, to take the picture of the roadside sign at the end of the prologue, and accompanied me with enthusiasm on a little road trip to Chambersburg, the Kennedy Farm, and Harpers Ferry in September of 2024. I would also like to thank my good friends Jennifer Waggenspack, Luke Mitchell, and Adriel Garcia, Esq., for reading drafts of the manuscript and giving me feedback and encouragement. Thank you all for your help.

I endeavored to ground this work in historical fact, and each of the events depicted herein is taken from the historical record. Osborne Anderson not only escaped from Harpers Ferry, he quite literally lived to tell the tale, publishing a memoir called *A Voice from Harper's Ferry* in 1861, which informed the account of Albert's and Osborne's escape.[1] The raid on Harpers Ferry, as well as the events at the Kennedy

---

[1] This work is in the public domain. I found a copy at historyisaweapon.com.

Farm and in Chambersburg, are also informed by this text, as well as two others which I would recommend to any reader interested in learning more about John Brown and the raid: *John Brown, Abolitionist: The Man Who Killed Slavery, Sparked the Civil War, and Seeded Civil Rights* by David S. Reynolds (Vintage Books 2006), and *Midnight Rising: John Brown and the Raid that Sparked the Civil War* by Tony Horowitz (Picador 2012). Professor Reynolds's book served also as the primary text for Albert's participation in John Brown's escape across Iowa to Canada, as well as a secondary source for the raid at Little Osage. In 2020, a high school teacher in Indiana, Pennsylvania, named Spencer Sadler published a biography of Albert called *Absalom Hazlett: A Loyal Soldier in John Brown's Army* (America Through Time 2020), which served as a source for the sign dedication described in the prologue, and informed descriptions of Albert's family and life on the farm in Pennsylvania.

In addition to these books, I also was able to find numerous old newspaper articles in the U.S. Library of Congress's "Chronicling America" archive, which provided several contemporaneous sources.[2] The narratives of Albert's termination from his job on the canal by Mr. McGovern for theft, as well as his subsequent arrest for horse theft in New York and agreement to testify against his accomplices, are based on an account of his early life published in the *Daily Appeal* (based in Memphis, Tennessee) on November 18, 1859. The rescue at Fort Scott, including Albert ("Haslett" in the article) having been grazed by a bullet, is based on an account of the event published in the *Daily Morning Leader* (Cleveland, Ohio) on January 10, 1859, an article published in the *Lynchburg Virginian* on January 6, 1859, and an article published in the *Shepherdstown Register* (Shepherdstown, Virginia) on May 29, 1859. The primary source for the account of the raid at Little Osage was an account published in *The Prairie News* (Okolona, Mississippi) on January 20, 1859. John Brown's escape to

---

[2] chroniclingamerica.loc.gov

Canada with freed slaves was informed by an article published in the *Randolph Journal* (based in Winchester, Indiana) on March 24, 1859. The description of Albert's arrest and habeas corpus proceedings in Pennsylvania was informed by an article published in *The Press* (Cincinnati, Ohio) on October 31, 1859. Aaron Stevens's background is informed by Professor Reynolds's book and an article published in the *Daily Morning Leader* on March 26, 1860. The trial and sentencing of Aaron and Albert is based on an account published in the *Daily Morning Leader* on February 26, 1860. Their execution was described in the *Cincinnati Daily Press* on March 23, 1860. Their burial in Perth Amboy, New Jersey, was described in an article published in *The Liberator* (Boston, Massachusetts) on March 30, 1860, and the need for a new burial location was described in an article in the *Daily State Journal* (Topeka, Kansas) on May 17, 1895. The epilogue about their reburial and the public ceremony in North Elba, New York, was informed by an article in *The Evening Star* (Washington, D.C.) on August 30, 1899.

There are also various other online materials that informed this book. The description of the sign dedication in the prologue was informed by an article on TribLive.com, a news website serving western Pennsylvania, on April 28, 2012. The scene of John Brown's ceremony on the eve of the raid is informed by an article by Robert L. Tsai, Esq., published in Volume 51, Issue 1, of the Boston College Law Review on January 1, 2010, called *John Brown's Constitution*. The maps and the picture of Albert all come from a booklet published by the U.S. National Park Service in 1974 called *John Brown's Raid*. Information regarding the reburial ceremony in New York came from an article published by the West Virginia Department of Arts, Culture and History in 2021 as part of an on-line exhibition on John Brown,[3] and an article by Pamela Merritt called *John Brown's Other Bodies* which was published by

---

[3] archive.wvculture.org/history/jbexhibit/jbchapter12.html

the town of Saranac Lake on its website in 2015.[4]

Sprigg Singleton Lynn and his family own the Kennedy Farm, and they have poured immense resources and endless care into preserving the site at their own expense. When I stopped with Amanda on our road trip, Mr. Lynn was mowing the lawn and, when he saw me, offered to take me on a private tour of the farmhouse, which I of course accepted. Thank you, Mr. Lynn, both for your preservation work and for the private tour. The property and farmhouse both look immaculate.

The Franklin County Historical Society owns the Ritner Boarding House in Chambersburg, Pennsylvania, and offers tours to the public, and I thank my volunteer tour guides for showing me around the place. I'm also grateful to U.S. taxpayers for supporting the U.S. National Park Service, which maintains the engine house and other historic sites in Harpers Ferry and exhibits them to the public. Finally, much of John Brown's dialog consists of scripture from the King James version of the Bible, so acknowledgment is due to King James and his army of scholars for creating it.

---

[4] www.saranaclake.com/story/2015/10/john-browns-other-bodies

ABOUT THE AUTHOR

Carl L. Engel is a writer and translator living in Philadelphia, Pennsylvania. He has published translations of *Professor Dowell's Head* by Alexander Belyaev and *Macunaíma: The Hero Without Any Character* by Mário de Andrade. *Clouds Tumbled into the Valley* is his first work of original fiction.